THE WARMTH OF A KISS

"As I told you earlier, you should ask young Gray if he knows of your engagement," Mr. Belvedere said.

"I suppose you are referring to his compliment to me, which you most unchivalrously referred to as 'false coin'!" Elise retorted. "I would remind you, sir, that you yourself said much the same thing to me just the other evening!"

"I remember that very well, Miss MacGregor—but the difference is that I do not deal in false coin. I say what I mean."

Elise, fully prepared to do battle for Mr. Gray's honor, had just opened her mouth to speak when she inexplicably found herself folded within Mr. Belvedere's arms.

"Nor do I require a kissing bough!" he announced, and pressed his lips to hers.

Elise stiffened and prepared to resist, but she suddenly realized that she did not wish to. The warmth she felt rushing through her and the tingling sensation, as though she had long been cold and had suddenly come to the fire's warmth, were completely unfamiliar and completely overwhelming. After a moment, she slipped her arms around his neck and returned his kiss warmly. . . .

Books by Mona Gedney

A LADY OF FORTUNE

THE EASTER CHARADE

A VALENTINE'S DAY GAMBIT

A CHRISTMAS BETROTHAL

A SCANDALOUS CHARADE

A DANGEROUS AFFAIR

A LADY OF QUALITY

A DANGEROUS ARRANGEMENT

MERRY'S CHRISTMAS

LADY DIANA'S DARING DEED

LADY HILARY'S HALLOWEEN

AN ICY AFFAIR

FROST FAIR FIANCÉ

Published by Zebra Books

Frost Fair Fiancé

Mona Gedney

ZEBRA BOOKS
Kensington Publishing Corp.
http://www.kensingtonbooks.com

AUTHOR'S NOTE: Although I have taken liberties with the precise timing of the weather events in this story, the blinding fog and blizzard, along with a Frost Fair, did occur in London in the winter of 1813–14.

ZEBRA BOOKS are published by

Kensington Publishing Corp.
850 Third Avenue
New York, NY 10022

All Kensington titles, imprints and distributed lines are available at special quantity discounts for bulk purchases for sales promotion, premiums, fund-raising, educational or institutional use.

Special book excerpts or customized printings can also be created to fit specific needs. For details, write or phone the office of the Kensington Special Sales Manager: Kensington Publishing Corp., 850 Third Avenue, New York, NY 10022. Attn. Special Sales Department. Phone: 1-800-221-2647.

Zebra and the Z logo Reg. U.S. Pat. & TM Off.

First Printing: May 2003
10 9 8 7 6 5 4 3 2 1

Printed in the United States of America

Prologue

For centuries, fairs have meant a world of color and excitement, amusement and entertainment, adventure and romance. A fair is also, however, merely a temporary world, existing for only a matter of weeks or even days. When the fair closes, the world disappears.

But that is not always true. . . .

One

"You are going to marry Robert Westbrook?"

Olivia stared at her sister in astonishment. Then her expression suddenly eased and her dark eyes lit with laughter as she dropped her reticule onto a table and removed her stylish little bonnet trimmed with cherries, smoothing her bright curls into place.

"Marry Mr. Westbrook! You are hoaxing me, Elise—and you very nearly took me in with your serious manner! Marry Mr. Westbrook, indeed! What a jolt you gave me!"

Elise smoothed the skirt of her blue-sprigged muslin gown, the only nervous gesture she would allow herself. She could not give way to emotion at Olivia's first response to the news. The two sisters were a study in contrasts. Everything about Olivia was vibrant and vivid—her golden hair and dark eyes, her volatile spirits, her quick and energetic movements. Everything about Elise, on the other hand, was calm and understated—her chestnut hair and blue eyes, her unruffled manner, her smooth and unhurried bearing.

Elise shook her head firmly. "I am not hoaxing you, Livy. I am as serious as ever I could be. The match is made, and the wedding will be in March. Mr. Westbrook spoke to Papa last Tuesday, and I accepted his offer."

The laughter faded and Olivia sank down beside her upon the sofa, staring at her sister as though she had taken leave of her senses. Elise sighed and patted Olivia's hand. This was going to be every bit as difficult as she had feared.

"But how can such a thing be true, Elise?" Olivia demanded. "I was gone only a fortnight to Chester, and when I left there was no mention whatsoever of Robert Westbrook—and certainly you had no thought of marrying him, or you would have said something to me! I know that he stood up with you at Mrs. Everly's ball last month, but that was not such a great thing! He danced with old Mrs. Granby, too."

Her eyes filled with tears and she shook her head in disbelief as she looked intently at Elise. "Why, such a match is impossible! He is decades older than you are!"

"There's no need to exaggerate, Livy," Elise replied calmly, determined not to let Olivia's response to the engagement overset her. She had known how her younger sister would receive the news, so she had steeled herself for the inevitable scene. Elise had often reflected that Olivia could have taken the place of Mrs. Siddons onstage, for she dramatized even the smallest happenings in their lives. She was incurably romantic and just as incurably outspoken. It could be a most trying combination, Elise reflected ruefully.

"Well, I am certain that he is at least fifteen years older than you!" maintained Olivia stoutly. "And that's far too great a gap between you! I cannot think why you would even consider marrying him!"

Elise attempted once more to reason with her. "Well, I must marry someone, and you know that he is a wealthy man, my dear—"

"And what has that to say to anything?" interrupted her sister. "Papa has money, too, so you need not marry strictly for fortune."

"Actually, Papa thinks that an important consideration," replied Elise, clearing her throat uncomfortably at

Olivia's shocked expression. "You and I do have generous dowries, of course, but he pointed out that there is the estate to think of, too. Since our land marches with Mr. Westbrook's, he would naturally have a vital interest in caring for it well. After Papa's death—I know it is terrible to talk about such a thing," she said hurriedly, looking at her sister's face, "but Papa brought up the matter, and you know how much he loves our home."

Their father's state of health was precarious, but the sisters never spoke of the possibility of his death, or of what that would mean to them. Elise, however, had decided that, as the elder sister, it was her responsibility to marry so that her future at least was secured. Their father would rest more easily knowing that she was taken care of and that she and her husband would care for Olivia should anything happen to him.

Mr. MacGregor was a man of modest fortune and, happily for his daughters, his property would not pass from the immediate family upon his death, even though he had no son. When he and his own father had drawn up a new deed of settlement at the time he reached his majority, Evan MacGregor had had the foresight to make an important change in it. Because of this, although he had no sons, his estate would be held in trust for his eldest grandson, provided that grandson took the family name of MacGregor. Unlike most entailed land, it would not go to the closest male relative in the absence of sons. However, the deed of settlement also provided for the absence of a grandson. If Mr. MacGregor died before there was an heir and no grandson was born by the time Olivia, the younger daughter, was twenty-five, the property would pass to the nearest male relative, a distant cousin living in Cumberland.

Elise cleared her throat and continued with determination, avoiding Olivia's eyes. She knew how callous and distasteful all of this seemed to her sensitive sister. "Papa explained to me that they had reached an agreement. After his death, the land will be under Mr. Westbrook's care, but it will be held in trust for our first son, to whom it will truly belong. It is a comfort to Papa to know that the land will unquestionably go to his grandson and that he will be taught to care for it properly."

At the mention of the child, Elise had colored deeply, but she continued sturdily, "Papa feels that Mr. Westbrook would be a good steward for the land, since he knows it so well and since he is a careful man." She made no mention of what would happen if she had no son, at which time the onus of providing one would fall upon Olivia.

An ominous silence descended as Olivia continued to stare at her in disbelief. She seemed to be waiting for Elise to continue, so Elise added, somewhat feebly, but with an attempt at briskness, "So you can see, Livy, that everything will work out very neatly."

"I see nothing of the sort!" retorted Olivia, rising to pace about the room, stopping at intervals to study Elise as though she were some peculiar and extremely unattractive new form of life. "What I see is that you have quite lost your good sense!"

"Marrying a gentleman of property and good birth whose respectability is known to us is an eminently sensible thing to do, Livy, whether you may think it so or not. If I were running away to marry a half-pay officer I had met at a county ball, you might then be permitted to think me a lunatic. What I am doing indicates a goodly degree of common sense."

"But we don't really know Robert Westbrook!" insisted Olivia, her brows drawn together and looking quite ferocious. "He may be our neighbor, but when have we exchanged more than half a dozen words with the man? For all we know, he might have a fierce temper and subject you to unspeakable treatment once he has you in his power!"

"Nonsense! I told you, Livy, that you have been reading far too many Gothic novels. I am not being kidnapped by some unknown villain who is carrying me away to a haunted castle. I am marrying a gentleman of good reputation who has lived next to us all our lives. If Mr. Westbrook were capable of the kind of behavior you describe, we should have heard of it from his servants long ago." Her sister needed little to fire her overactive imagination, and a steady diet of stories by Mrs. Radcliffe had caused her to suspect dark secrets in the most innocent of households.

"What have servants to say to anything?" Olivia demanded. "Mr. Westbrook has never been married before, so we do not know how he might behave with a wife!"

Elise was well aware that there was some validity to Olivia's fears, but she would not admit it to herself. Society made few provisions for the security of women. Unless their fathers made special legal arrangements for them prior to marriage, everything they owned belonged to their husbands. Mr. MacGregor had explained to Elise that he had discussed with Mr. Westbrook the matters of her pin money, her jointure should Mr. Westbrook predecease her, and generous portions for any children they might have. A legal agreement attesting to these would be drawn up and signed before the marriage. Elise knew that she had been generously provided for—but she also knew that once she married, she was entirely in the power of her husband. A wife had no rights of her own as an individual; she had to obey her husband, whether he beat her or treated her like a duchess. By law, she would belong to him, as would their children.

Elise tried not to think of such things, for there was no

profit in it. When such thoughts arose, she reminded herself that Papa had those same rights, and she and her mother and sister had always been treated well. She had no reason to believe that Mr. Westbrook would do otherwise.

"A man such as you describe would also treat his servants badly and his horses, too, simply because he has the right to control them, and you know very well that Mr. Westbrook does no such thing," replied Elise firmly. "You are simply letting your emotions and your imagination run away with your common sense."

"Well, one of us should feel some emotion, and it is a certainty that you do not!" snapped Olivia. "Otherwise you would never shackle yourself to some unknown, elderly man for the sake of his money!"

Elise overlooked the sudden change in her characterization of Mr. Westbrook from villain to a doddering old man with one foot in the grave and focused instead on this newest accusation. "Livy! How unjust you are being! You know very well that there is no truth in what you are saying!"

"Indeed! Then pray explain to me just what you *are* doing!" Olivia retorted.

Elise paused, then replied slowly, "I am marrying a gentleman who will secure my future and that of my family."

"You see!" exclaimed Olivia. "It is just as I said! You are marrying an unknown, elderly man for the sake of his money! You are merely dressing it up in fine words!"

For a moment Elise pictured what Mr. Westbrook's expression would be if he were to hear himself described as elderly, and she shuddered. He was an active, vigorous man, actually quite an attractive one, but his manner was unquestionably abrupt and he was accustomed to having his way without any interference. It would be difficult to keep Olivia from saying something outrageous directly to him, and that would make their lives together much more difficult. Her sister was dear to her, and she would not wish her to alienate Mr. Westbrook so that she made herself unwelcome in his home.

"Come now, Livy, do be reasonable," she coaxed. "I don't wish for you to be angry with me."

Elise suddenly realized that she was speaking to an empty room, however, for Olivia had rushed into the passageway in a stormy frenzy of sobbing. In a moment she heard the door to Livy's own chamber slam behind her.

She sank into a chair, sighing deeply and absently fingering a brown curl that had pulled loose from the ribbons that held her hair in place and now dangled against her cheek. There was no good in trying to reason with her sister at the present moment. Long experience had taught her that once Livy had worked herself into a passion, several hours had to pass before there was any hope of rational conversation. It was up to Livy to make the next move.

The afternoon passed slowly, although Elise kept herself busy with needlework and took a brisk walk to attempt to restore her peace of mind. Walking always improved her spirits, even when the wind chilled her to the bone as it did today.

She had reminded Olivia of how their father loved the land upon which they lived, but the truth was that she loved it dearly, too. High above her rose Finnian's Hill, the site of a beacon fire, the wood still ready to light at the first news of an attempted sea attack by Bonaparte. Even though no one truly expected such an attack now, a pot of pitch had been kept ready over the years. Two hundred years earlier, such a fire had been lighted here, one of a chain of fires that blazed across the country, warning the people that the Spanish Armada had been sighted off the Cornish coast.

Elise passed Barrow Lodge, a venerable stone building

that had stood for over two hundred years. It had been here when the signal fire warning of the Spanish had been lighted. Beyond that lay St. Stephens, a chapel built in the fifteenth century, destroyed by the Roundheads, and lovingly restored by the people after the return of Charles II.

Here they were always aware of their deep roots in the past. Farmers tilling their fields regularly turned up coins, shards of pottery, jewelry, and other evidence of life in medieval times, in Roman Britain, and in times even earlier than that. Elise smiled, remembering a lovely looking glass she had discovered while planting bulbs in their garden at Brookston Hall, one used by some young woman fifteen hundred years ago. She had taken it to her father, who had inspected it, recorded its description in an album he kept, cleaned it carefully, and put it away, as he did with all such discoveries.

She stopped for a moment at the entrance to Mr. Westbrook's estate, Harrington Hall. The wrought-iron gate stood closed, forbidding callers, and she knew that the gatekeeper waited in his gatehouse to inspect those who wished to enter there. She knew that beyond the gate lay a winding avenue leading to the hall through sycamores and lime trees, and that at the end a carriage sweep would leave guests at the front door of the Jacobean mansion. And she was to be mistress of this.

Quietly she slipped by the gate so that she would attract no attention and, turning down a narrow lane, she climbed over a stile and took a path that led through a copse to home. Restored by her walk, she was able to greet her sister cheerfully. Dressed in a warm scarlet pelisse, bright against the gray of the December day, Olivia was waiting outside for Elise at the entrance to the shrubbery walk, and they linked arms companionably and entered one of their favorite hideaways. When they reached the heart of it, they seated themselves on the stone bench there, comfortably protected from the brisk winter wind by the high hedges.

They had walked together silently, but it had been a peaceful silence. However, after they were seated on the bench, Olivia looked Elise directly in the eye and said, "There is no shame in crying off should you change your mind, Elise. No one else knows of the engagement save us and Mr. Westbrook, do they?"

Elise shook her head. "We did not wish anyone else to know until you came home and I could tell you."

Olivia nodded her head in satisfaction. "And what could be more natural than a young girl suddenly realizing that she has acted in haste? No one else would know of your change of heart, and Mr. Westbrook would get over it soon enough, for assuredly his affections are not engaged."

"To be certain, his heart is not engaged," Elise agreed, "but I fear that his pride might be injured by such an act—and he is a very proud man, you know." The image of Robert Westbrook coolly asking her for her hand, already certain of what her answer would be, remained vivid in her mind. He had been every inch the gentleman, but she had been keenly aware that he felt he was bestowing a great honor upon her.

She sighed. And it was, of course, an honor. Becoming Mrs. Robert Westbrook would make her a woman of considerable standing in their rural society. More than that, it would secure her father's peace of mind. Since she had never expected to make a love match and had found none of the young men she had met particularly engaging, she was the logical one to marry him. Her sister's disposition would never allow such a match for herself. Indeed, Elise had sometimes worried that Livy might do something mad, like eloping with a half-pay officer.

Olivia leaped upon both her words and her sigh. "You

see!" she exclaimed. "It is just as I said! Already he is op-
pressing your spirits, Elise, and you have just admitted
that he is stuffed with pride!"

"And why should he not be?" asked Elise reasonably.
"He is a handsome man of good family and solid fortune. I am fortunate to be making such a match."

"*He* is fortunate, also!" said Olivia sharply. "You are an
attractive, well-bred young female with a respectable fortune of your own—and the pleasantest disposition in
Christendom! He should be grateful to be your husband!"

Elise laughed. "Perhaps I should tell him so," she
replied, attempting to establish an easier tone. And, she
realized unhappily, such a tone would be even more difficult to achieve with the stern and distant Robert
Westbrook.

"So you should! I daresay that he felt that he was hon-
oring you with his proposal, with never a thought
beyond that!"

"I believe most gentlemen must feel that way when
they make an offer, Livy." Sometimes Olivia, although
usually sharp-witted, seemed very slow to understand the
obvious. "If a man has family and fortune, you surely
would not expect him to be apologetic and profess himself to be unworthy of a lady."

"Any gentleman would do so if he were in love with
the lady in question—or even if he simply recognized
her worth!" Olivia insisted, her color growing higher by
the minute. "If he valued the lady properly, he would
naturally make it clear that he would consider himself a
most fortunate man should she accept him! Indeed, he
should say that he is not worthy of such a prize!"

"Livy, Livy, you have read too many novels," Elise chided
her gently. "And, of course, *you* have Arthur Townsend,
who is so entirely smitten with you that he would walk
across coals of fire for a single dance. We cannot all be so
fortunate." Surely, she thought, the mindless devotion that

so annoyed her sister would divert her attention for at least a moment or two.

Olivia's cheeks grew more crimson still. "Never mind Mr. Townsend!" she protested. "He is just a boy!"

Arthur Townsend, a fresh-faced young man newly graduated from Oxford, would have been crushed by this observation from his goddess. He had fallen top-over-tail in love with Olivia when he had come to visit friends in the neighborhood, but he had been kept at arm's length by her father. Although their country society was informal, Olivia was still too young to have a train of admirers. However, even had her father permitted young Townsend's attentions, she would still have scorned them, having told Elise that he looked precisely like a sheep when he looked at her.

"And you are still just a girl," her sister reminded her, her tone still gentle. "You need not worry about the attentions of Arthur Townsend, nor about choosing a husband. Those are matters that you need not trouble yourself about just yet, and you will understand them better by and by."

Despite her words, Elise was not at all certain that Olivia would ever see courtship and marriage in the practical light that she herself did.

"Honestly, Elise, you make it sound as though we are separated in age by a decade! I will soon be sixteen and you are scarcely two years older! Don't behave as though you are my grandmother!"

Elise sighed. "But I often feel as though I am," she confessed. "You know that I have none of your romantic notions, Livy. I have never cried over the sad tales of lovers like Romeo and Juliet or Tristan and Iseult as you have, because to me they are just that—stories, not life. And, since I lack your sensibility, I must do what seems wisest for me. I shall marry Robert Westbrook, who is a fine figure of a man, though he is older, and I shall make him a very good wife." She turned to Olivia and hugged her. "Can you not wish me happy, Livy, and promise me that you will stand by me?"

Olivia, her cheeks streaked with tears, returned her hug tightly. "You know that I wish you happy, Elise—and that is why I don't want you to marry him."

"But if I assure you that marrying Mr. Westbrook will make me happy?" Elise asked, leaning back so that she could look her sister in the eye.

"Then I suppose I must believe you," said Olivia reluctantly, the words fairly wrung from her. Then, with her normal passion, she embraced her sister tightly once more. "And if you are not happy, Mr. Westbrook will have to answer to me!"

"That will have him quaking in his boots!" laughed Elise, feeling that she had finally made some headway. She knew that the struggle with her sister was not over by any means, but the worst—she trusted—was behind them.

Wisely, she had saved her trump card for this moment. "And, Livy, Papa says that we are to go to Aunt Ravinia in London to choose my bride clothes." Their father, a widower, seldom left his country home, and their rare visits to the home of his older sister had been prized by both girls.

"London!" breathed Olivia reverently. "When are we to leave?"

"Almost immediately," said Elise promptly. "Papa has already written to her that we will be there in time to take Christmas dinner with them. He will escort us there and then come back here to complete the arrangements with Mr. Westbrook."

To her great relief, Olivia was so caught up in the thought of going to London that, for the moment at least, her unhappiness with the marriage was put aside.

Arm in arm, the girls rose and made their way back to the house, talking eagerly of the trip to come.

Only after Olivia was asleep that night was Elise able to think over her situation in peace. She had been startled when their father had told her of Mr. Westbrook's request for her hand in marriage, but she had already given careful consideration to the matter of marriage in general and had decided what her course of action must be. Her father was a kind man, so he would never force her to marry a man that she disliked, but Elise had no objection to Mr. Westbrook as a suitor. Despite Olivia's protests, she was fully conscious that being chosen by such a man was a mark of distinction. She should be proud, for she knew that countless young women had set their caps for him. She had not, and he had chosen her.

She smiled to herself a little as she thought of Livy's demand to hear an account of the proposal itself. Predictably, she had been horrified by its utter lack of romance.

"Why, he might as well have sent his man of business to make the offer!" she had protested, her cheeks scarlet with indignation after Elise had finished the story.

"Yes, but he did tell me that he had long observed me, Livy, and that he felt, despite my extreme youth, that my gracious, sensible behavior—and those were his very words, my dear, so you can see that he respects me—would make me an enjoyable and suitable companion." Elise's eyes were bright with amusement.

"Now there is an ardent tribute indeed!" exclaimed Livy, outraged. "I wonder that he did not ask for a letter from Papa that guaranteed your ability to do sums accurately so that you can keep your household accounts. Perhaps he should quiz you on your knowledge of housekeeping and servants so that he may be assured you can keep his establishment running comfortably!"

"Well, as a matter of fact, we did discuss what some of

my duties would be," Elise conceded, adding, before Livy could raise another outcry at such behavior, "and you know that such concerns are very necessary to address. Everyone does so."

"But not in a proposal! His behavior shows a complete disregard for your feelings!"

"On the contrary," responded Elise, "I feel that he honored me by making clear his expectations of a wife— and by telling me, too, what I can expect of him. I know that I shall always be treated with respect, that I shall receive a very generous allowance, that we shall go to London once each year, and that I shall have my own carriage at my command." Here she patted her sister's hand encouragingly. "So, you see, he is not planning to enslave me, Livy dear."

"You shall very likely die of boredom!" sniffed her sister, unimpressed. "There will be no magic in your marriage!"

Clearly, Olivia had not been mollified by her explanation of the situation, but she had at last let the discussion go and Elise had turned their conversation to the pleasures of a visit to London, so the evening had ended pleasantly enough. Although she was by no means reconciled to the marriage, by the time they retired to their separate bedchambers, Olivia was at least no longer openly railing against it.

As Elise prepared for bed, she allowed herself the luxury of thinking about what she would like to do, rather than what she should do. Mr. Westbrook and Harrington Hall played no part in her vision. Instead, she saw herself in London, visiting Ackermann's, driving through Hyde Park to see not just the park but the members of the *ton* taking their pleasure there, strolling down Bond Street, enjoying a confection at Gunter's. She could picture it all so easily, and she looked forward to being able to indulge herself in such unaccustomed pleasures, even for a brief time. For the moment those were enough for her. They would make a splendid change of pace from her daily life. Home was all very well, and she acknowledged to herself that she loved it, but it would be delightful to have such a change.

She had not yet managed—or even attempted—to picture herself as Mrs. Robert Westbrook. There would be time enough for that when she returned home from London. As she drifted at last into sleep, she attempted to conjure up an image of Mr. Westbrook's face, but she found herself totally unable to do so. Curious, she thought, when she had known him all her life.

Ah well, she assured herself, she would work on that tomorrow—or perhaps, better still, after her trip to London. She thought of Livy's indignant protest that she would have no magic in her marriage. Her last thought was of relaxing at Gunter's with a lemon ice after a day of shopping. That would be magic enough for her.

Two

To the sisters' delight, their father was as good as his word, and only two days later they began their slow progress to London, pausing three times at posting inns so that Mr. MacGregor could rest. He had fallen victim to a weakness of the lungs four years earlier, and the disease, even though it periodically loosened its grip on him, had still taken a heavy toll on his stamina. Olivia fairly bounced with impatience at the delays, but Elise reminded her quietly that traveling was difficult for their father.

"Oh, I know, Elise," she sighed. It was early afternoon on their first day of travel, and the two girls were in the chamber they would share that night. "I would never say anything to hurt him—you know that I would not! And I do know that we must stop even though there are hours of daylight left when we could travel. It's just that I fairly *burn* to get there! Don't you feel the same way, Elise?"

"Indeed I do," she answered, smiling. "And soon enough, we will be. I have been entertaining myself by imagining all the things that we will do and see—and how delightful it will be to spend time with our aunt and her family."

"We shall have a splendid time!" agreed Olivia, her eyes bright in anticipation. "I know that Nigel and Monty will take us everywhere we wish to go." Nigel and Monty were their cousins, both polished young gentlemen of the *ton*.

When they finally arrived in London two days later, they made their way to Darlington Square, where Ravinia Longfellow's handsome home occupied a major portion of one side. She had married well, and her husband had left her and their children a comfortable fortune. Her home was a most welcoming sight, for light shone in all the windows. The curtains had not yet been drawn against the gathering night, and Ravinia herself opened the door and swept past the butler, hurrying down the steps to greet them. Not far behind her came several members of her family, calling to the MacGregors cheerfully. It had been almost a year since their last visit to London, although they had been urged to come more frequently and to stay for a longer time when they did come. This time Elise and Olivia were to remain for several weeks, although their father planned to return home the day after Christmas, leaving Elise and Olivia to stay with his sister until the end of January.

"But you have scarcely arrived, Evan," Ravinia complained when he assured her that he would indeed be making so brief a visit. Their trunks had been taken upstairs, and they had settled comfortably in the drawing room. "Why must you be so stubborn? You know that you need to rest for a longer time before you begin the long journey back—and you will miss all the holiday festivities."

Ravinia Longfellow was a tall, imposing woman, and she was a woman accustomed to having her way. She had been a widow for almost fifteen years, but her children had always assured Elise and Olivia that even when her husband, Lionel, had been alive, she had been the dominant force in the household. Nor did they doubt it for a moment.

Her brother, however, was not to be browbeaten. The long years of illness had left him much paler and far less vibrant than Ravinia, but Evan MacGregor was still capable of firm dealing.

"And you know very well, Ravinia, that resting in your home is well nigh impossible. In fact, I shall do well to survive the visit," he replied, smiling to take any sting from his words.

"A home truth, Uncle," chuckled Monty, patting Evan appreciatively on the shoulder and grinning at his mother. "Needn't leave this house for entertainment. Makes me think of Astley's—except there's no need to buy a ticket to it."

He waved his arm to encompass the whole of his mother's elegant—and very busy—drawing room. All of her family was with her for the holiday, and her grandchildren were enjoying themselves hugely. Five-year-old Nelson was riding his stick horse round and round the perimeter of the room while his twin brother, Niles, practiced his tumbling act over the back of a large brocade sofa. Their younger sister, Tillie, perched on a low stool, was rolling a ball that a small tan and black terrier patiently and repeatedly retrieved for her, dropping it into her lap each time. The mother of these three, Ravinia's daughter Sally, sat watching them fondly, occasionally cautioning Niles to be certain that his flying boots did not strike the dog.

Ravinia's sharp-tongued daughter-in-law, Lucy, was also watching this display, obviously irritated by it. Since Ravinia allowed it, there was little she could do about it, however, which irritated her still more. Her husband, Charles, oblivious to everything about him, was deep in his newspaper, and she knew it would do no good to appeal to him anyway, for he would only shrug and say that there was no harm in it. She reflected bitterly that the twins could be setting fire to the room so that they all went up in a puff of smoke and he would still shrug and see no harm in it—or at least not until his newspaper caught fire.

Lucy's two older sons, Reginald and Theodore, well aware of their mother's opinions about proper behavior and mindful of the holiday treats that could be withheld, were calmly playing chess in a remote corner of the room, far removed from potential danger, while Lionel, the youngest son, sat at her knee looking at a picture book. Marjorie, Charles and Lucy's only daughter, was seated at the pianoforte, playing a medley of Christmas carols.

Evan smiled at his nephew. "You have described it very aptly, Monty," he replied. "This does put me strongly in mind of my last visit to Astley's—which was some years ago, of course—and I believe that Nelson might have a promising future there. I daresay he could mount any horse that they have and ride it around the ring a dozen times."

"Should think the poor beast would drop dead long before Nelson slowed down," observed Monty astutely. "Could likely go through three or four horses before he broke a sweat."

"Well, I think that a little liveliness would be just the thing for you, Evan," said Ravinia. "It would be good for you to have something interesting going on about you. That would take your mind off your ill health. I know that you need rest, but surely you do yourself no good by living such a very secluded existence. *Do* stay with us a little longer."

At this moment Niles, having brought his boots down rather too sharply on his little sister's head, suddenly gave up acrobatics for his stick horse and joined his brother in circumnavigating the room, Nelson circling it in a clockwise direction, Niles riding counterclockwise. Bangs the terrier decided to join them, running first with one, then the other, barking sharply all the while. Tillie, clutching her head and sobbing, was being soothed by Sally.

"I do thank you for the very tempting invitation,

Ravinia," Evan responded, gazing about the room in amusement, "but I think the only thing I must consider now is whether I should leave immediately."

"For the love of all that's holy, Mama!" exclaimed a dapper young man standing in the doorway. "Can you not send these hellions up to the nursery so that we may have a civilized conversation—or at least so that I do not go deaf at a tender age? I waited until dark to return in the hope that they would all have been put to bed."

"Nigel! Where have you been?" cried Olivia, flinging her arms around the neck of her favorite cousin. "I was devastated that you weren't here when we arrived!"

"I would have been here had I known just when to expect you. I've been spending rather more time than usual at the club," he replied, hugging her and winking at Elise. He raised his quizzing glass and glanced around the room, then shuddered. "For some reason, I have found it a little more restful than home."

Nigel was the only one of Ravinia's children who still lived at home. He had finished at Oxford the previous year, and she had thus far managed to keep him with her. He was the picture of a young dandy, his hair perfectly arranged to achieve artful disorder, his neckcloth high, stiff, and immaculate, his jacket exquisitely tailored. Monty, who was four years older and also considered a most eligible young bachelor, had rooms of his own on Duke Street.

Nigel glanced at his sister, Sally, and shook his head. "Edward said to send you his best, Sally, and to tell you that he will be here within the hour. I persuaded your husband that he cannot live at the club, no matter how desperate he is to avoid the chaos here."

"Come now, Nigel, don't exaggerate," said Ravinia, patting his arm. "You will distress Sally."

"No, Nigel cannot manage to do that, Mama," responded Sally lightly, looking anything but distressed as she neatly scooped up Bangs before he could make the critical error of welcoming the newcomer by pawing Nigel's exquisite biscuit-colored pantaloons. "He has been trying to ruffle my feathers for days, but he hasn't been able to do so. No doubt he has estimated how long he thinks it will take him to anger me and placed it in the betting book at the club."

Wagering about virtually anything had been a popular pastime among gentlemen of the *ton* for years. In the betting books were recorded wagers made by members, along with the dates, the amount of the wagers, and their outcome.

Nigel kissed her lightly on the cheek. "You are brilliant, my child," he assured her. "I had not thought of recording this as a wager. I shall do so immediately. There should, after all, be some profit in suffering."

Here he turned to Elise and embraced her warmly. "And I understand that I am to wish you happy, my dear girl. Tell me about the fortunate man. Is he handsome? Did he sweep you off your feet?"

"Hardly!" exclaimed Olivia bitterly, her comment winning raised eyebrows from the adults of the assembly.

"Robert Westbrook is a gentleman that I have known for years," inserted Evan calmly. "Elise is making an excellent match."

"And so is he!" said Olivia sharply.

Her father ignored her tone and merely nodded. "Naturally," he agreed, "and Mr. Westbrook is keenly aware of his good fortune."

"Should hope he is," replied Monty earnestly. "Shall tell him so if he's in doubt, for it's important he understand it." Here he paused to glance at Olivia with a troubled expression. "Is he?"

"Is he what?" asked Nigel irritably. "I do wish you would work on expressing yourself more clearly, Monty!" Monty was at home to a peg in all matters concerning fashion, and he was considered a very pretty whip, but many, other than his closest companions, occasionally had trouble in following his conversation.

"In doubt," returned Monty, undeterred.

"Of course he is not," replied his uncle, a little crossly. "Naturally Mr. Westbrook is aware of Elise's value."

"Certainly he is aware of her value," agreed Olivia. "Our land marches with his," she said to the others by way of explanation.

Her father's thin face flushed. "That is not what I meant, Olivia, as you are well aware."

"I don't mean to distress you, Papa," she said quickly, "but you must admit that this is a very convenient marriage for Mr. Westbrook."

"And for us as well," he reminded her.

"I greatly regret that you never saw fit to allow me to take Elise for a Season, Evan," said Ravinia. "It would have been an excellent thing for her to acquire a little town bronze and to look about a little before marrying and settling down."

"You know that Papa would have allowed me to come, Aunt Ravinia, but I could not bring myself to do so when his health was once more so uncertain—and of course now that I am to be married in March, my situation is different."

"Married! An awful thing, that," said Nigel, shuddering delicately. "Leg-shackled for life. Don't do it, my girl! Run while you still can!"

Evan MacGregor was looking increasingly unhappy. "I don't think that you should make it sound as though this marriage is a terrible thing. Elise will be treated well and she will have a good life with Robert Westbrook. I know the man."

"It may be a good marriage, Papa," returned Olivia, although her tone cast doubt upon that statement, "but it will certainly be a drab one. She will be living in almost the same place and seeing all of the same people and doing all of the same things that she has done all of her life!"

"Quite shocking," agreed Ravinia, who preferred the lively life in London, while Nigel and Monty looked horrified by this bleak picture of Elise's future. Even Sally, who was occupied with removing a Chinese vase from Nelson's grasp and restoring it to safety, looked taken aback.

"I'm certain that Elise is simply grateful to have made a good match," observed Lucy. "That is a most important consideration for a woman. She needs to marry well so that she has some security. It is not necessary that she also be entertained." Here she glanced significantly at her husband, Charles, who was still deeply engaged with the newspaper.

"Evan, you must send Olivia to me for the Season," Ravinia announced decisively. "It is too late for Elise, of course, but we may still be able to do something for Olivia."

A sudden flurry of activity from the corner of the room broke up the conversation. Niles had crawled atop a chest and catapulted himself into the middle of the chess game, and bedlam ensued. The adults most nearly concerned hurried over to round up the children and bundle them off to the nursery, while most of the remaining adults took advantage of the moment to flee to their rooms and dress for dinner.

When calm was restored, Charles remained, still reading his paper, Monty stood next to the fire, for he had already dressed for dinner at his own lodgings, and Elise stood next to him, staring into the flames.

"Feeling quite the thing, Elise?" he asked, concerned. "Not having an attack of the megrims, are you?"

"No, Monty," she replied after a moment had passed. "No, I'm quite all right. Thank you for asking, though. You are a dear." She smiled up at him and patted his hand.

Reassured, he returned her smile. "Best go and change

your frock," he suggested gently. "Wouldn't do to sit down to dinner in a travel-stained gown."

"No, of course it wouldn't," she said absently, turning toward the door. "Thank you for reminding me."

"Happy to be of service," he called after her, and turned back to the warmth of the fire.

Elise made her way slowly up the stairs, still hearing Olivia's words ringing in her head. *Livy is correct,* she told herself. She would indeed be living in the same place she had always lived, seeing the same people she had always seen, and doing the same things she had always done. Marriage would bring very few changes to her life. Much as she loved her home, she had not stopped to think of her future in these terms. Suddenly everything sounded very dull—and very final.

And what was it her aunt had said? *It is too late for Elise.* She knew that her aunt had been referring to the Season and husband-hunting, which was now no longer necessary for her—but it sounded very like an announcement of the end of everything. *It is too late for Elise.*

And Olivia would be coming to London for the Season. She would undoubtedly capture the heart of some fascinating gentleman who would prize her above everything and give her an interesting life. They would travel everywhere and see everything. And Elise would be trapped at home, without even Livy for company.

She began to rub her temples. Perhaps she was coming down with a case of the megrims after all.

Three

"Well, isn't this much better?" inquired Nigel cheerfully at dinner. "Here we are, actually able to hear one another speaking so that we can hold an intelligent conversation. Isn't this a much more desirable arrangement than the scene of bedlam in the drawing room?"

All of the children had been consigned to the nursery, and only the adults in the family—with the exception of Evan, who was taking his meal in bed—had reassembled.

"Is it?" inquired Sally dryly. "I suppose that would depend upon whether or not we want to hear what everyone else is saying."

Monty looked puzzled. "Can't very well have a conversation if you can't hear what's being said," he pointed out reasonably.

"Just what I was observing," said Nigel. "You are right on target, Monty. Naturally we must hear what others are saying if we wish to converse with them."

Sally glanced at him as though she would like to do him violence, but she said nothing. Her children were a very sensitive point with her. Unlike many mothers of her class, she chose to spend a great deal of time with her offspring, rather than leave them entirely to the tender mercies of a nanny, no matter how excellent.

"Of course, it is much easier to have a respectable conversation when the children present are all well behaved," Lucy pointed out, her tone and expression virtuous in the extreme. Lucy was also very proud of her children, particularly of Reginald, the heir, although she spent less time with them than Sally did with hers. She was known to be the only disciplinary force in the family, the one who withheld rewards as well as dispensed punishments, and the children kept that well in mind. "It is most important, I believe, to teach children how to conduct themselves in a manner that will bring credit to themselves and to their parents." Her words and her sharp glance at Sally indicated clearly how far short she felt her sister-in-law fell in this respect.

"And I would like to point out, Lucy, that all of your children, with the exception of Lionel, are at least five years older than Niles and Nelson. Any comparison is most unfair. As I recall, at the age of five Reginald and Theodore were not angels either."

"Still not," inserted Monty abruptly. When he realized that everyone was looking at him, he added, "Angels, that is." He paused a few moments longer, gathering his thoughts, then continued. "Fact is, Charles, meant to speak to you about them yesterday."

Lucy had begun to bristle at Monty's first comment, her thin lips tightening ominously, but Charles was paying no particular attention to the conversation until he heard his name.

"What's this, Monty? You wanted to speak to me? About what?" He put down his paper for a moment and gave his brother his full attention.

"About Reginald and Theodore," returned Monty. "No sense of propriety. Deuced near got me killed yesterday."

At that, everyone looked up, and Ravinia spoke. "But I see that you are here with us, my dear, without any visible injuries."

"Said 'almost,' Mama," he returned briskly, then

turned to appeal to Nigel. "That's what I said, ain't it, Nigel?"

His brother nodded impatiently. "Do go ahead and tell us what happened, Monty."

"Bamboozled me into taking 'em up in my curricle," said Monty, his expression dark. "Had to crowd a bit, but they're not oversized. Told me they wanted to see London Bridge, so we tooled off to the city to have a look-see."

"But what is wrong with that?" demanded Lucy. "They merely wanted to ride in your curricle and see the sights of London."

"Rocks!" returned Monty briefly. Then, seeing that the others did not comprehend the enormity of what he was saying, he added, "Brought rocks in their pockets and chunked 'em at a pieman and a coal wagon before I saw what they were about!"

He closed his eyes, as though reliving the awful scene. "Traffic was nose-to-tail, moving like molasses, so the pieman had time to catch us. Had a bloody kerchief pressed to his forehead and was kicking up such a dust that everyone to Covent Garden could hear him. Made me cut a pretty figure," he added bitterly.

"What about the coal wagon?" asked Charles, interested for the first time that evening. "Did the driver notice the rocks? Nasty tempers, some of those wagoners."

Monty shuddered. "Saw the fellow get out of his cart. Probably a blacksmith—had hands like hammers! Could have threaded me through the eye of a needle if he'd had a fancy to do it."

"But obviously he didn't," observed Charles. "How did you outfox him?"

Monty rubbed his fingers together. "Rolls of soft," he explained. "Hate to waste the ready, but hate to be threaded, too."

"Well done!" exclaimed Charles, impressed in spite of himself. "Some men would have fainted or run away, Monty, but you stood your ground."

Monty shrugged. "No choice," he said simply. "Had no place to go or would've run like a hare. Couldn't leave my cattle."

"You should have remembered to check the boys' pockets, Monty. After all, they are only children," Lucy pointed out. "I daresay you'll remember to do so before you drive them out next time."

Monty's eyes fairly started from his head. "Next time? Shan't be a next time, Lucy. Daresay you all think I'm a sapskull, but I'm not such a gudgeon as to take out that pair of devil cubs again!"

"They only wanted some attention," Lucy protested. "They need to spend time with a gentleman. They do so enjoy it."

"Charles," replied Monty briefly. "Best be with their father." Several of the others nodded in agreement.

"They are with me at home," said Charles firmly, not overanxious to spend more time with his brood. "What they need here is to be with their other relatives, establish family ties, that sort of thing."

"That would leave Elise, Olivia, Sally, and Edward," announced Nigel briskly. "The rest of us spend quite enough time together, and we have already established our ties, thank you. As I recall, you and Lucy spent a fortnight with us just this autumn."

"Do be serious, Nigel," said Lucy crossly. "The children's feelings are very important to me."

"I assure you, I am being perfectly serious," he replied. "My own feelings and the peace of the household—to say nothing of Monty's health—are very important to *me.*"

"Well, perhaps I should say that I too am very concerned about *my* children's feelings," said Sally, looking from Nigel to Lucy. Seeing the apprehensive expressions of the others at her words, she smiled fleetingly, then turned on the hapless Monty. "What do you say, Monty? What about taking up Niles and Nelson in your curricle tomorrow? You would not wish to appear to favor one set of cousins over another."

Monty's expression was that of a fox cornered by the hounds. Then, apparently being visited by some over-whelming emotion—probably caused by a sudden vision of the driver of the wagon of coal, thought Elise—his shoulders straightened and he spoke firmly. "Not possi-ble. Thinking of my health, you know," he added hurriedly.

"Oh, for heaven's sake, Sally, leave poor Monty alone," said Charles irritably. "You and Lucy can take all of 'em to a puppet show. Let 'em get to know their cousins bet-ter and form their ties with one another." He grinned briefly. "Serve 'em right."

Monty's shoulders sagged with relief. If Sally and Lucy felt somewhat less relieved, they had no opportunity to mention the matter. Ravinia stepped in to redirect the conversation, which had begun to annoy her as well. She was inordinately fond of her grandchildren, despite their faults, but she did not choose for them to be the focus of all discussions.

"Fortunately, we shall be spared this sort of digression at Christmas dinner tomorrow, both because we shall have the children at table with us and because we shall have guests," she announced, looking pleased.

"Guests?" inquired Sally. "Shall there be anyone that I know?"

"I don't believe so, my dear. Two of them are friends of Nigel who find themselves in town without family to go to for the day."

"You may not know them, Sally, but our cousins know at least one of the gentlemen in question," added Nigel, looking at Elise and Olivia. "I believe that you are acquainted with Arthur Townsend. He said that he paid a visit to a friend of yours earlier this year and made your acquaintance then."

"Yes, he certainly did," responded Elise, injecting the appropriate amount of interest into her voice and glancing briefly at Olivia. This was not the time for her sister to voice an opinion of Mr. Townsend. "It will be very pleasant to see him once more."

She had apparently conveyed her caution to Olivia, who satisfied herself with merely nodding, then asking, "And who is the other gentleman, Nigel? Is he also someone that we know?"

Nigel shook his head. "James Gray has not yet met you, but after Townsend's glowing description of the two of you—which I did nothing to correct, you understand, no matter how overly enthusiastic it was—he is most certainly looking forward to making your acquaintance."

Elise avoided looking at Olivia's face to see her reaction to this statement and hurriedly inquired about the identity of the other guests. Ravinia informed them that the only other guests apart from Mr. Townsend and Mr. Gray would be Colonel Bradley, a retired officer who was a friend of Evan, and Mrs. Fotheringale, a friend of her own.

Despite the misgivings of some of the adults, particularly Monty, Christmas dinner went smoothly. All of the children, even Tillie, were in attendance, and Bangs sat close beside her, patiently awaiting any tidbits that might come his way. Even Evan, who was still gray with fatigue and annoyed by the presence of young Townsend, enjoyed the company, particularly that of Colonel Bradley.

"You see, Evan," said Ravinia triumphantly, as the dinner wound to a close, "you really should spend at least a few more days with us. That would give you and the colonel time to renew your friendship properly."

"Yes, do stay, MacGregor," agreed the colonel. "We haven't had a chance to talk in years. I would be glad of the opportunity."

Mrs. Fotheringale, who was also acquainted with him, nodded her agreement so enthusiastically that the ostrich feathers in her hair bobbed as though they had taken on a life of their own. Elise, who had been enjoying both the lady's conversation and her dress—she still wore the powdered wig and patches and gown popular three decades ago—listened to the interchange with amusement.

"Yes, by all means stay, Mr. MacGregor," said Mrs. Fotheringale, playfully tapping his arm with her fan, which she carried despite the wintry weather. "Ravinia speaks so highly of you that I would be pleased to know you better—and then, of course, I have always had an eye for a handsome man. Did Ravinia mention to you that my fourth husband died last year so that I am once again an eligible widow?"

Evan chuckled and shook his head. "No, she did not. But no matter how much I should enjoy improving our acquaintance, ma'am—and spending time with you, Colonel—I fear that I must hold to my plan and depart tomorrow."

"I am glad to know, Miss MacGregor, that at least you and your sister will be remaining in London," said James Gray, smiling warmly at Elise, who was seated next to him. "I now have something to brighten my thoughts during the dull winter days."

He was, she thought, a delightful young man. His appearance was pleasing, his intelligence quick, his manners impeccable. She had discovered that he was a few years older than Nigel, who had been a companion of his younger brother at Oxford.

"I am sorry that our father's health forces him to return home so quickly, but I must confess that we are looking forward to our stay here," she replied, returning his smile.

"I trust that you will allow me to do what I can to help you enjoy your visit," he returned. "Townsend had described you and your sister to me in very striking terms, but I fear he did not manage to do you justice. Even Nigel who, as you know, rarely compliments anyone, assured me that his guests were most charming."

Monty, who had heard the last part of this, leaned toward him confidentially. "Think Nigel meant just Elise and Olivia," he said in a low voice. "Best to keep your distance from the rest of 'em."

Mr. Gray looked puzzled by this comment, and Elise said in explanation, "I believe that Monty is suggesting that you keep your distance from the rest of the houseguests— more than likely from the younger guests."

Monty nodded in confirmation. "Rocks," he said to Mr. Gray briefly. "Never take 'em out in your curricle."

Then, satisfied that he had done what he could to preserve the life of a fellow creature and a guest of the house, he returned to his dinner.

Mr. Gray looked more lost than ever, and Elise chuckled. "Monty had a quite hair-raising experience with some of the children," she said in a low voice. "I shall tell you about it later, if you like."

"And I shall look forward to that moment," he assured her warmly.

Ravinia rose from the table then, a sign to the ladies to leave the gentlemen to their cigars and their port. The children also repaired to the drawing room with them for the evening's entertainment. Marjorie made her way straight to the pianoforte and began her repertoire of carols as the others made themselves comfortable.

The drawing room, like the rest of the house, was garlanded with Christmas greenery in honor of the season, with even a kissing bough, bright with berries, hanging high in one of the doorways. A comfortable fire flickered in the fireplace, its glow lending warmth to the room, the Adam chimneypiece lending grace. Despite the fact that pastels were all the rage, the walls of the room were a deep shade of gold. Feeling very much at ease, Elise seated herself and prepared to relax, even in the presence of a gaggle of energetic children. Marjorie's cheerful rendering of "Deck the Halls" had for the moment captured them, and they were singing together, except for Tillie and Bangs, who sat together and watched the others.

The gentlemen, with the exception of her father, who had retired early, appeared much more quickly than she had expected, and joined the others in singing "The Holly and the Ivy." At the close of it, Marjorie, pink-cheeked, curtsied to an enthusiastic round of applause.

"Will you play for us next, Miss Olivia?" inquired Arthur Townsend, who had taken his place beside her despite her best efforts to avoid him. "What a pleasure it would be to hear you sing."

"If you'd heard Livy sing, you'd know that's a thumper," announced Nigel brutally. "It's Elise who sings."

The unfortunate Townsend looked startled at this unchivalrous comment, but Olivia, long accustomed to her cousins, merely laughed and agreed. "Nigel's quite right. It's Elise we want."

Elise, who did not care for performing, would have liked to refuse, but she could see no gracious way to extricate herself from the situation. Then James Gray turned to her and smiled.

"I hope that you will favor us with a song, Miss Mac-Gregor. Do you know 'Green Groweth the Holly'?" he asked. "That is one of my favorites."

Elise inclined her head and allowed herself to be led to the pianoforte, where most of the children were still gathered. To her pleasure, Mr. Gray placed himself so that he could see her face. Gently she began the old song that he had asked for, which was one of her own favorites.

> *Green groweth the holly,*
> *So doth the ivy,*
> *Though winter blasts blow never so high,*
> *Green groweth the holly.*
>
> *As the holly groweth green*
> *And never changeth hue,*
> *So am I, ever hath been,*
> *To my lady true.*
>
> *As the holly groweth green*
> *With ivy all alone,*
> *When flower cannot be seen,*
> *And greenwood leaves be gone:*
>
> *Now unto my lady*
> *Promise to her I make,*
> *From all others only*
> *To her I me betake.*
>
> *Adieu, mine own lady,*
> *Adieu, my special,*
> *Who hath my heart truly,*
> *Be sure, and ever shall.*
>
> *Green groweth the holly,*
> *So doth the ivy,*
> *Though winter blasts blow never so high,*
> *Green groweth the holly.*

When she had finished, there was a warm round of applause.

"What a lovely piece," sighed Olivia. "Such touching sentiments by a true lover." Here she darted a glance at her sister to be certain that Elise had taken her meaning and realized that such a phrase did not describe Mr. Westbrook, but Elise appeared unperturbed.

"Yes, it is just what you would expect a faithful lover to say," agreed James Gray, his eyes also on Elise. She flushed slightly, but she was not required to respond, for her cousin Charles suddenly decided to contribute his mite to the conversation.

"Interesting to think that they believe Henry VIII wrote that, isn't it? Gives rather a different flavor to the whole thing."

Monty goggled at him. "Henry VIII?" he demanded, his voice rising in disbelief. "Fellow that was fat as a flawn and faithless? *He* wrote it?"

Charles nodded. "As I said, knowing that he wrote it makes it sound a bit different, doesn't it?"

"But the blighter had six wives!" Monty protested. "And thought nothing of chopping off the head of one so that he could have another!"

Nigel laughed. "I suppose he could have sung it to each of them and meant it—at least for the moment."

"Well, it is *still* a lovely song, Nigel, no matter how horrid you choose to be about it!" said Olivia, ruffled by the discussion.

Nigel patted her on the shoulder and made an uncharacteristically generous remark. "Livy, dear, I have no doubt that any gentleman singing that to you would mean every word of it."

Before she could enjoy the compliment, however, it was spoiled by the ever present Arthur, who said in a voice vibrant with emotion, "Indeed, you are correct. I can only wish that I could sing. I would prove it to you myself, Miss Olivia."

Nigel, encountering Livy's horrified glance and feel-

ing somewhat responsible for such an unwanted out-
pouring, responded quickly, "But since you cannot,
Townsend, by all means let us have Marjorie return to
the pianoforte and favor us with one last round of 'The
Holly and the Ivy.'"

Marjorie gladly resumed her place and soothed any
lingering distress with that favorite carol. As she watched
the others, Elise reflected that Nigel was much more
perceptive than she sometimes thought him. After all,
who could harbor ill will when singing such a carol?

> *The rising of the sun*
> *And the running of the deer,*
> *The playing of the merry organ,*
> *Sweet singing of the choir.*

The words died away, and for the moment peace was
restored to their little world. Coffee was served with an
assortment of sweets, ostensibly for the children, although it was clear that the grown-ups were enjoying
them, too.

To the delight of the children, their grandmother
then distributed their Christmas boxes to them, each
child receiving a gift of money from her. When everyone
had eaten and drunk as much as was possible, Ravinia
announced that it was time for the children to go up to
bed. Their protests were many and heartfelt, but she remained firm. In the face of much pleading, however, she
allowed them to gather round Marjorie at the pianoforte
for one more resounding chorus of "Deck the Halls."

While the others were thus engaged, James Gray, who
had caught Elise's arm when she rose to join the others
at the pianoforte, bent toward her and whispered, "May
I have just a moment of your time, Miss MacGregor?"

"Certainly, sir," she responded, pleased at the opportunity to spend a minute or two in privacy with such a charming man.

He guided her toward one of the doorways of the far end of the drawing room, slipping something from his pocket as he did so. As they reached the doorway, he held out his hand, a golden locket glowing in his open palm.

"I wanted to show you this," he said, clicking open the locket with a flick of his thumb. "It is a miniature of my mother."

Elise studied it for a few moments. A delicate, hopeful young woman looked back at her, large-eyed and wistful.

"She is lovely," murmured Elise, touching the edge of the golden case gently.

"And so are you, Miss MacGregor," he whispered, his lips suddenly close to her ear.

Startled by his nearness as much as by his words, she glanced up at him and looked into his smiling eyes. Dark-eyed like his mother, she thought, as he leaned toward her. A proper young woman, particularly a proper young woman who was engaged, should turn and walk away, she told herself.

His lips met hers gently but firmly, and his hand cupped the back of her head, holding her closer, while the other held her waist lightly. So sweet was it, and so natural, that she wished that he would never move.

When he did, he looked down into her eyes once more and smiled again, this time merrily. "I could not resist, Miss MacGregor. Pray do not think ill of me for taking advantage of the season." And here he glanced up at the kissing bough above them.

A sudden commotion from the other end of the room announced that their activity had been noticed. Above the hooting of Reginald and Theodore, she could hear Monty saying plaintively, "Don't need a kissing bough when there's no one here but family."

That turned out to be an unfortunate oversight on his part, for Mrs. Fotheringale announced firmly, "I'm not family, Monty! Come along!" And she briskly dragged him the length of the room and kissed him soundly, to the applause and laughter of the others. Even Bangs entered into the merriment, barking jauntily and making brief runs at Monty's ankles.

All in all, Elise thought, as she pulled the covers up to her chin that night, it had been the most pleasant Christmas Day that she could recall. It was because of the family and frolic, of course—it was merely a coincidence that the vision of James Gray's face appeared each time she closed her eyes.

It had been a most satisfying day.

And she had not thought, even once, of Robert Westbrook.

Four

When Elise awoke the following morning, she was filled with a curious feeling of lightness. It was not merely that her spirits felt lighter at the memory of a pleasant evening, but also that her very body seemed more buoyant. When she walked downstairs to the breakfast room, it seemed to her that she must have shed many pounds overnight, for she was aware of a sensation of quickness and grace that she had never known before.

Nor did it seem that the change was entirely in her mind. As she entered the breakfast room, Nigel's eyebrows rose. He, Monty, and Charles were the only three gathered there.

"Need I ask, dear cousin, just what has brought this glow to your cheeks and spring to your steps? Or is it entirely a private matter, too personal to share?" he inquired.

"I am merely responding to the day. It is indeed a lovely day, isn't it, Nigel dear?" she replied brightly, serving her plate from the sideboard and seating herself beside Monty, who had come from his own lodging at this unseasonably early hour so that he could bid his uncle farewell.

Monty stared doubtfully out the window at the swirling gray fog, much of it caused by the smoke produced by the thousands of London homes warmed by coal fires.

"Shan't say you don't have the right to your own opinion, cousin," he said, "but it seems devilish dreary to me. Very nearly went directly back inside this morning when my man opened the door on such a miserable mess."

"It is simply a case of beauty being in the eye of the beholder," returned Elise, sipping her chocolate cheerfully.

"And I wonder just what has made this particular beholder so very willing to see beauty in a morning such as this," said Nigel, eying her thoughtfully.

"Could be right," observed Monty, who had been considering her comment. "Not entirely dreary. Children are still in the nursery. Enough to brighten the day right there."

"You see," said Elise with satisfaction, "it is all in the way you look at things."

"And where is Livy?" asked Nigel. "One would think that she could come down and share her sunshine with us as well."

"She had just awakened as I left. She will be down shortly, for she won't wish to miss having breakfast with Papa before his departure."

"She is probably afraid to come down for fear Townsend is lurking in the drawing room, ready to lay his heart at her feet again," said Nigel. "And he'd be here, too, if he could think of any pretext that would justify his appearance at this ungodly hour."

Evan MacGregor and Ravinia entered just then, so the conversation took a different turn, and Elise was grateful that for the moment she no longer had to fend off Nigel's curiosity. She had not yet attained safety from observation, however, for her aunt regarded her for a moment, then spoke.

"You are in uncommon good looks today, Elise—very animated."

"Thank you, Aunt," she replied demurely, noticing that her father had looked up sharply. "I suppose that I am simply pleased to be in London. And I am most certainly looking forward to going out today, despite the weather."

"Where do you plan to go?" inquired Ravinia. "My carriage is at your disposal. Are you wishing to begin shopping for your bride clothes immediately?"

"Ah, perhaps that is the reason for your bright good looks this morning," said Nigel. "You are thinking of the delights of preparing for your wedding. Nothing warms the feminine heart more than spending vast quantities of money."

Elise felt her smile fade, but she knew her father was watching closely, so she restored it immediately. She had not been thinking at all of bride clothes or her marriage, but she could not say such a thing.

Ignoring Nigel's comment, she replied, "As a matter of fact, Aunt, I had thought that I might wait a week and begin my serious shopping after the New Year. I had hoped that perhaps we might be able to take a drive through town, and then stop and stroll along Bond Street, just to look."

"Take you in my curricle," offered Monty promptly. "You and Livy will fit, for you're small—but no children," he added darkly, glancing at Lucy, who had just come in and seated herself beside Charles.

"Do stop being such an infant, Monty," said Lucy, her voice quite as sharp as her chin and her nose. "It will be heartless of you to turn your back on Reginald and Theodore simply because you were careless. You could easily take them on a brief ride before you take Elise and Olivia."

Monty's eyes bulged. He was normally the best-natured of men, but Lucy brought out the worst in him.

Elise hurried into speech before he could reply. Ignoring Lucy, she said, "We would love to go with you, Monty. I can think of nothing more delightful."

"Yes, nothing quite like a brisk ride in a curricle on a cold, foggy day," agreed Nigel dryly. "It sounds heavenly. If your luck is in, perhaps it will snow, too."

Mention of the weather diverted the conversation as Ravinia turned to her brother. "I have bricks heated for your carriage, Evan, and I had Beavers take the lap robes in by the kitchen fire so that they are properly warmed, too. I do hate to see you leave in such miserable weather."

Evan smiled at her. "Thank you, Ravinia, for looking after my comfort so well. As to the weather, you know that it is simply what we can expect of the winter."

Ravinia shook her head. "It seems to me much colder than it usually is at this point in the year—but then perhaps it is merely because I am growing older."

"Nonsense, Ravinia," her brother replied. "You do not look a day older than you did ten years ago. You seem to be one of those fortunate people who never age."

And what he said was not mere flattery, Elise reflected. Her aunt's hair, although laced with gray, was still enviably dark and thick, her skin unlined and clear, and her posture erect. Most certainly her strength of will and her level of energy would have put most people of any age to shame. She was clearly a force to be reckoned with.

Ravinia's eyes softened at this unexpected tribute from her younger brother, but she responded briskly, "Nonsense, Evan! You are merely trying to get round me with soft words, for you know that I wish you to stay instead of going out into such weather. It cannot be good for your health!"

Olivia appeared at this moment, creating a diversion that her father took full advantage of, directing the conversation to the discussion of what she and Elise would do during their weeks in London, and an animated discussion followed.

"I shall return for you at the end of January, so do not

make yourselves too comfortable here," he reminded the girls, as the household turned out to see him tucked securely into his carriage. When Elise bent forward to kiss him good-bye, he spoke to her in a low voice.

"You will watch over your sister?" he asked her earnestly.

"Of course I shall, Papa," she assured him.

"I rely upon your good sense. I do not like it that young Townsend is underfoot," he said. "I don't wish for her to become involved with him."

Elise laughed and whispered, "You needn't worry, Papa. Livy can scarcely bear the sight of him. He will be fortunate if she speaks a dozen words to him."

Her father's expression relaxed, and he was able to bid his daughters farewell with complete composure and begin his journey home. After Ravinia had cautioned his coachman no fewer than five times to watch himself carefully in the fog, to mind the potholes, and to stop at an inn the instant his master tired, Mr. MacGregor was able to take his leave.

Elise and Olivia returned to the house, shivering from the cold, but eagerly making arrangements with Monty for their outing.

"You are quite mad, you know," Nigel informed them. "This is a day for staying by the fire. If I go out, it will be to the club, where they have a fire equally as warm."

The sound of children thudding down the stairs caused him to pause. "Upon second thought, I shall indeed go to the club, where they will feed me and keep me warm, and where I may indulge myself in civilized pleasures with other adults."

"I do look forward to the day when you have several children of your own, Nigel," remarked Sally. "I shall enjoy it above all things."

He shuddered gently. "Don't be ridiculous! I shall

never marry," he assured her. "I can only be grateful that I could learn my lesson vicariously."

The occupants of the nursery swept past them, crying their good mornings and ignoring Sally's questions, and hurried on toward the billiards room.

"How extraordinary! Are they that excited to play billiards?" asked Olivia, startled by their enthusiasm.

Charles came strolling down the stairs, his greatcoat over his arm. "I told them that Monty was waiting for them there, and that he planned to take them on an outing. In the meantime," he said, slipping into the coat with the aid of an attentive footman, "I am leaving for the club."

"You are a brilliant man, Charles," said Nigel in admiration. "Wait for me and I shall go with you."

"You'd best be lightning quick," replied his brother. "At the faintest sign of their return, Beavers will open the door and I will be instantly gone."

Ignoring Sally's protests, the gentlemen hurried away and Elise and Olivia, grateful that they, too, were making their escape, went upstairs to prepare.

"Perhaps we should send a footman to wait outside at the corner to tell Monty not to come in," observed Olivia as they changed.

Elise laughed. "Surely you don't think that we need to be so extreme, Livy," she replied. "We can simply tell the children that there isn't room in the curricle."

"Do you wish to explain that to them?" asked Olivia. "And do you wish to see Monty's expression when the horde descends upon him the instant he walks into the house? We will never catch him. He will be gone in an instant."

Elise reflected a moment. "Perhaps you have a point," she agreed. "But we won't send a footman. We'll wait outside for him ourselves. Monty is always prompt, so we won't be there long, and the children won't set up a cry to come with us."

Accordingly, a few minutes later, the sisters slipped quietly out the front door, aided by Beavers the butler, who closed the door after them stealthily, and together they hurried to the corner to watch for Monty.

"At least we will not have to feel that we are drawing attention to ourselves, two solitary ladies waiting on a street corner," said Elise, glancing round them as they established themselves. Wisps of fog swirled about them, often concealing what was merely a few feet away. "In this weather no one will notice us."

As though to give the lie to her words, she heard her name called. Turning quickly toward the sound, she saw James Gray emerge from the mist. Her heart leaped at the sight of his already familiar form, tall and elegant, striding toward them.

"Miss MacGregor! How good to see you—to see both of you," he added, noticing Olivia and bowing to them both. "I was just on my way to call upon you, although I realize it is still early. I had hoped to be able to pay my respects to your father before he left."

"How very kind you are!" she returned, surprised and pleased that he should take such trouble. "He would have appreciated that very much, but I fear that he has already departed."

He smiled ruefully. "I was afraid that would be the case," he replied, "but I didn't wish to arrive at dawn with the milk carts. That would have been far too forward, even were I an old friend."

Before Elise could reply, he offered his arm, saying, "Forgive me, ladies, for keeping you standing here in such abysmal weather. May I offer to escort you to your destination?"

"In truth, Mr. Gray, we are waiting here for our cousin Monty. We have an appointment to ride out with him."

James Gray looked puzzled. "But certainly he expects to come to the door for you. He would not ask you to wait for him here, particularly in such foul weather."

"No, of course not," Elise assured him. "Monty's manners are impeccable. It is simply that the children will set upon him if he comes into the house. He does not know that they are waiting, and I fear that he would be horror-struck."

Gray, who had heard the story of Monty's agonizing outing with Reginald and Theodore, laughed heartily. "Then you are assuredly performing an act of Christian charity," he assured them. "I don't believe his shattered nerves could withstand another youthful assault."

At this happy moment, Monty's curricle appeared through the fog, a trim, well-polished vehicle pulled by two well-matched bays. Upon being hailed by the group on the corner, he drew up smartly, and stared at them in consternation.

"Thought I was to fetch you at the house," he said, puzzled. "Change your mind about riding out with me?"

"No, indeed," Elise assured him. "But the children are lying in wait for you inside, so we thought that we would try to save you from them."

Monty threw a terrified glance in the direction of the front door, which was curtained from their view by the fog. "Be a good fellow and hand 'em up quickly, Gray," he urged. "Reginald has the nose of a hound and he'll be out here directly even if he can't see us from the house."

Still laughing, James Gray helped up Olivia and then Elise, holding her hand a moment longer than necessary and saying in a low voice, "I shall call again, very soon, ma'am."

"Sorry to rush, Gray, but it's an emergency," said

Monty, tipping his hat in that gentleman's direction. "Hope to do you a kindness in return."

The ladies scarcely had time to thank James Gray before Monty had urged the horses into motion and the curricle pulled away into the fog as quickly as safety would allow.

Elise turned to wave, but the figure of Mr. Gray was already lost in the folds of gray. She turned around and sighed in contentment. She could still see his merry face, enjoying the comedy of their predicament. And she had no doubt that he would soon put in another appearance in Darlington Square.

"Mr. Gray is most attentive," observed Olivia as they pulled away. Casting a sidelong glance at her sister, she added, "I daresay we shall be seeing a great deal more of him during our visit."

Refusing to be led into further discussion of this dangerous subject, Elise replied sedately, "I hope we shall. He seems a most agreeable gentleman."

"Good fellow, Gray," agreed Monty. "Could have been caught by the terrors if he hadn't gotten the two of you into the curricle quickly. Quite a tight squeeze here, too. Can you breathe, Livy?"

Olivia laughed. "Yes, but we are very snug. It's fortunate that all three of us are on the slender side. If not, one of us would have to perch on the groom's seat."

She poked Elise gently with her elbow. "You will not be doing such things as this once you are married to Mr. Westbrook," she said. "You shall have to be very dignified and serious, and I daresay you will spend your days sitting in front of a fire, dutifully mending stockings—and perhaps netting a purse or reading an improving book as an extraordinary diversion."

"You are too harsh, Livy. Remember that I told you I shall have a carriage of my own," Elise replied, but she felt some of the lightness of the morning leave her, and a decided heaviness begin to settle in her midsection. For a moment Mr. Westbrook's unsmiling visage rose before her, but she resolutely closed her mind to it. There would be time enough to face the future. "And at any rate, we shall talk no more of Mr. Westbrook or the wedding today. Today we are simply going to enjoy ourselves." If it occurred to her that Mr. Westbrook and her marriage to him could not be coupled with enjoying herself, she made no mention of it. Wisely, neither did Olivia.

"Right you are," said Monty approvingly. "Today we are on the toddle!"

Pinks of the *ton* were often "on the toddle," sauntering about town and appraising everyone and everything with a critical eye, often aided by a quizzing glass. Monty, although quite fashionable enough to be considered among that elite group, was far too good-natured to slash others to ribbons for the sake of his own ego. Neither Olivia nor Elise felt inclined to be critical, either. They were prepared to enjoy themselves immensely, pausing to study each trinket in Phillips before finally choosing with joy a pair of bracelets to be worn over long gloves, purchased for them by their obliging cousin. Together they debated the relative merits of lavender water and rose water, then inspected carefully the china on display at Wedgwood and Byerley's.

The fog did not lift as the day progressed, but instead grew much thicker. The shops along Bond Street and Regent Street lighted their windows, and the lamplighters put in their appearance much sooner than usual so that the streetlights also cast a yellow glow against the gathering grayness.

"It has been glorious, Monty! Thank you so much for squiring us about today," said Elise, sipping the last of her tea and leaning back in her chair to enjoy the unaccustomed luxury of taking refreshments in a confectioner's shop among people of fashion.

"My pleasure," he replied graciously. "But best get you back so that I've time to nip round to Duke Street and dress for the evening."

"Are you dining with us tonight?" Olivia asked hopefully. "Or are you planning to go out?" Family gatherings were always pleasanter when Monty was present.

"Out," he responded briefly, his eyes twinkling as their faces fell. "Going to the theatre. Got to send my man to pick up the tickets after I take you home."

"I hope you enjoy yourself," said Elise politely, preparing herself for an evening of maternal debate about the best methods of rearing children.

"Thought you liked the theatre," returned Monty in surprise.

"We do," said Olivia, looking at him in puzzlement.

"Then we'll all enjoy ourselves," he replied cheerfully. "Always liked The Great Grimaldi."

"Are we going with you?" demanded Olivia joyfully. "And Grimaldi is playing?"

Monty nodded in satisfaction, pleased with the reception of his surprise. "Taking Mama's coach. Nigel's coming along, too."

Olivia hugged her cousin impulsively, almost crowding him off the seat.

"Here now! Have a care!" he protested. "Don't wish to be dashed to the roadway, Livy! Can't very well go to the theatre if I'm in hospital!"

He managed to get all of them safely home, however, and as soon as he had helped them down from the curricle, he sprang back up and drove smartly off before the door could open and the horde of children descend upon him.

Five

Elise and Olivia arrayed themselves carefully for the evening, assisted by Ravinia's maid, who dressed their hair. Elise chose a blue sarcenet, trimmed in scarlet ribbons with a sash of the same color tied under her bosom, and flat leather slippers of the same scarlet.

"I know we shall be dreadfully out of style," Olivia fretted, studying her own white, green-beribboned frock in the glass. "I daresay everyone will know that we've come fresh from the country."

Elise laughed. "Perhaps so—but what do we care, Livy? Next week we shall outfit ourselves properly, for Papa promised that you shall have new gowns as well."

Olivia's face brightened at this. "You're quite right, Elise. I should not be complaining. After all, we *are* going to the theatre, and we are being escorted by gentlemen— just as though I was already out instead of a schoolgirl miss. Sarah will be wild with envy." Sarah Foreman was her favorite companion from Miss Skeffington's Academy for Young Ladies.

Remembering their father's request that she look after her younger sister, Elise said dampingly, "Yes, but recall that the gentlemen are our own cousins, Livy."

Olivia laughed and threw her arms around her sister. "You are right, of course, but, as you said, what do we care? No one else shall know it, and we shall appear to be two ladies enjoying an evening at the theatre in the company of two gentlemen who are delighted to be our escorts."

"Well, you may be stretching that a bit, my dear. I am trying to picture Nigel and Monty appearing overcome by our charms," demurred Elise, but she smiled as she slipped on the pair of bracelets Monty had purchased that afternoon.

"They will appear to be so," Olivia promised, "because I will tell them that I shall faint dead away if they don't pay us the proper amount of attention."

"Livy! You wouldn't do such a thing!"

"Of course I would," she responded briskly. "You know that I can make myself faint in an instant simply by holding my breath. Just imagine how mortified Nigel and Monty would be if I collapsed in the middle of the performance."

"I would be quite mortified myself," Elise assured her, "so I pray that you will not think of doing so, Livy. Very likely they would refuse to escort us anywhere else if you were to misbehave in such a manner."

That comment won her sister's attention, so Elise was comforted by the assurance that Livy would not be performing that evening and would allow the actors upon the stage to have that honor. She did not feel entirely certain of that, for one could never be absolutely confident that Livy would do as she was bid. However, Elise had done what she could, and she felt that her sister's desire to see London in the company of her cousins would keep her behavior in line.

Promptly at the close of dinner, the coachman brought round the carriage, and Nigel escorted them out into the foggy winter night. Their progress to Duke Street to pick up Monty and on to the theatre was slower than it might have been because of the density of the fog. The coachman threaded his way carefully through the traffic, but the coachlamps of other vehicles were often not visible until they were only a few feet away. Sounds seemed curiously muffled, and the scene took on an air of mystery.

Olivia shivered slightly, and leaned closer to her sister. "I'm very glad that I am not walking tonight," she said. "My heart goes out to those who must do so."

"Feel the same away about driving," observed Monty. "Glad it's John Coachman up top and not me."

"Why, Monty," said Olivia, surprised, "I had not thought that anything about driving troubled you at all. You seem so very sure-handed."

Monty flushed with gratification. "Good enough in my way," he admitted. "Member of the Four-in-Hand Club," he added proudly, referring to an exclusive group of excellent whips.

"Of course, even Prinny used to be good with a whip," observed Nigel, weary of the talk about driving. "I understand that he used to drive a high-perch phaeton with a team of six—but look at him now." The Prince Regent was now known more for the greatness of his girth, unsuccessfully restrained by corsets, than for his prowess as a driver.

"Here now, Nigel, are you hinting that I'll end up like Prinny? Just because you can't tell one end of a horse from another—" began Monty, severely ruffled.

"Of course he would not think any such thing," interceded Elise smoothly, throwing Nigel a warning glance. "There is a great deal more to being a gentleman than handling a horse well, Monty—and we all know that you are most truly the gentleman."

Mollified, Monty allowed himself to be led into more cheerful avenues of conversation, happily relating a prank that had been played upon another young man whose lodgings were close to his. While the young man was at his club, a group of his friends, with the aid of his valet, had moved all of his furniture and clothing from his rooms into a vacant lodging. The young man had, of course, been horrified upon his return home, and had been about to lodge a complaint in Bow Street when his friends made the truth of the matter known to him.

Laughter followed his tale but, after a short pause, Elise asked, "But I don't understand—why did they do that, Monty? What object did his friends have?"

The other three stared at her. "Why, to have a little sport," he responded slowly. "Don't you see? Something for them to do."

"They didn't have anything else to do?" she asked. "Surely there was something else. How do they spend their days?"

Nigel answered her, enumerating the items on his fingers as though he were saying his rosary. "Those with the proper connections spend their time in a variety of ways, cousin dear. They go to their clubs to gossip and gamble and dine; to Tattersall's to admire the cattle and display their knowledge of them; to 'The Sublime Society of Beef-Steaks' to watch the steaks cooked and eat them and drink arrack punch from pint pots; to the rooms of Gentleman Jackson to go a few rounds with the master; to Weston's to have their coats fitted; to Hyde Park to show off their cattle and their driving skills; to Vauxhall to meet their flirts; to Almack's to see the newest shipment of young brides-to-be for the marriage mart—"

"Nigel!" snapped his brother, calling him back to a sense of propriety and forcing him to remember his audience. After all, two of them were new wares for the marriage market, and the implication of his words was scarcely delicate.

"Forgive me," said Nigel in a repentant voice. "I do sometimes allow myself to get carried away. Suffice it to say, dear ladies, that they—or I suppose I should say we—remain constantly busy, but we are very busy about very little."

"I see," said Elise, although she truly didn't. Even Livy seemed subdued by Nigel's description of their lives. For a moment, the glamour of life in London seemed slightly tarnished.

Very shortly, however, they found themselves in the theater, caught in the excitement of a crowd. As Monty swept them along to their seats, Olivia's eyes grew larger by the minute. She had never seen such gowns, such jewelry, such fine gentlemen. Suddenly realizing that she was also the focus of admiring eyes, despite her country attire, she lowered her eyes and kept them fixed demurely on Monty's pumps as he led Elise to their places. Nigel held her arm firmly, as though suddenly aware of the need to protect her. Elise was equally aware of the glamour of the crowd, but, unlike Olivia, she was not subjected to the close scrutiny of admiring eyes.

To their delight, Monty had engaged a box, and the four of them settled themselves comfortably.

"You see, Elise, isn't this splendid?" demanded Olivia in a whisper. "How can you exchange pleasures such as this for the dullness of becoming Mrs. Robert Westbrook?"

Elise had no ready answer as she took in the scene from the box, which granted them an excellent view of both the stage and the audience.

"Missed the first act," Monty whispered, and they settled into a production of *The Farmer's Revenge* that was already under way. The four of them were soon engrossed by the trials of the humble farmer, whose lovely bride has been kidnapped on their wedding night by a villainous lord and who must face all manner of obstacles to win back his wife.

As the tale came to a close and the curtain fell for the final time before the pantomime, they were joined in the box by Arthur Townsend and James Gray, both of whom had called in Darlington Square, only to be informed by Beavers that the young ladies had gone to the theater.

"Told him to if Gray called for you," whispered Monty to Elise in a low voice. "Thought you'd want him to know."

Elise colored slightly and nodded, thinking that it was unfortunate that Mr. Townsend had also called at the same time. Olivia looked somewhat less than enchanted by his presence.

"Well, what do you think?" asked Mr. Gray, pulling his chair close to Elise.

"Of what?" she inquired, smiling. "The play? A little too dramatic for my taste, perhaps, but still enjoyable." She glanced about the theater at the colorful scene. "This is much more to my liking," she said. "I love to watch the audience. They have many tales to tell instead of just one."

His arm rested close to hers, and she was keenly aware of it. In a moment, his hand had clasped hers warmly, but he acted as though he were unconscious of this connection. With his free hand, he gestured toward the people below them.

"Show me what you mean, Miss MacGregor," he said. "Tell me a tale about one of the members of the audience." He leaned forward and studied those below them. "Her!" he said suddenly, indicating a thin elderly woman, dressed in black bombazine.

Elise looked down at her. "I shall call her Mrs. Taylor. She is here alone, so she has no family. Possibly she is a widow—thus the black—and has no children to support her. She is nicely dressed and her gown well-made, although somewhat worn. She is a gentlewoman, fallen upon hard times."

"Why is she here then?" asked Mr. Gray. "If what you propose is true, why would she be spending her money on the price of a ticket when she might be more in need of food or lodging?"

"Because she loves the color and drama and seeing the people," answered Elise promptly. "If she sat at home each night, she would be insupportably lonely, but here she is a part of a pageant of life."

Mr. Gray held her fingers to his lips and kissed them. "Thank you for the tale, Miss MacGregor. You have made me look at the world a little differently, and I am grateful."

Elise smiled, and she did not immediately remove her hand from his. It was interesting, she thought, that she had once laughed when reading that a young woman had drowned in her lover's eyes. How ridiculous she had thought the notion! And yet now she felt that catching her breath as she looked into his eyes was a most difficult—perhaps an impossible—undertaking. She would be less smug about love stories now. Olivia might have been more correct than she had believed.

Fortunately for Elise's peace of mind, the pantomime soon began, and her attention was held by Joseph Grimaldi, the consummate clown of the British stage, son of an Italian Pantaloon father and a Columbine mother. She had long heard of Grimaldi, who had exchanged the rosy cheeks of the harlequinade clown for a white face with scarlet half-moons on the cheeks and who had achieved fame in *The Golden Egg*, the Harlequin Mother Goose. Tonight he appeared as Dame Cecil Suet in *Pantomime of Dick Whittington*.

Not until the pantomime was over did Elise realize that Olivia had moved her chair between Monty and Nigel so that she would be free of the unwanted attentions of Arthur Townsend. Suddenly realizing she had forgotten her responsibility to care for her sister because she was so absorbed in her own happiness, she whispered a request to Mr. Gray to give his attention to Olivia. She herself distracted Mr. Townsend, determined to keep him fully occupied so that her sister could enjoy at least the final portion of the evening.

So successful was she that Mr. Gray remained by Olivia's side until their carriage arrived for them, and Mr. Townsend was forced to fade into the background. As they rode home through the fog, she was grateful to hear Olivia say gently, "This was a perfectly splendid night, wasn't it?"

The others readily agreed, Monty being especially pleased since the trip had been his own idea.

"A night at the theater can change the way you look at the world," Olivia added dreamily.

Elise was quite in agreement with her sister. It had indeed changed her view of the world. The unusual feeling of complete happiness that had flooded through her on Christmas Day was with her still, and she wanted to retain it. She had realized as she told Mr. Gray the tale about the woman in the audience below them that she too wanted to be a part of the pageant of life, not merely an onlooker.

She had made up her mind.

When she arrived back in Darlington Square, she was going to write to both Mr. Westbrook and her father before her head touched the pillow. Her father, she hoped, would understand. Mr. Westbrook would not.

There would be no wedding.

Six

It was late when she went bed to that night, but by the time she retired, the deed was done. Two letters, neatly blotted, folded, and sealed with a wafer of wax, lay on the desk. She stared at them for a moment, then slipped them into a drawer. Olivia had inquired sleepily why she was writing instead of coming to bed, and Elise had told her that she composing a note to their father. She had not mentioned Mr. Westbrook.

She had told each of them that she did not wish for the marriage preparations to continue. To her father, she had explained that even though she had been in London only a few days, the distance from home had allowed her to take a fresh view of the matter. She was now certain that marrying Mr. Westbrook would be a mistake. She had written:

> *While I had not necessarily expected to make a love match, having met Mr. James Gray, I now realize that it is indeed possible to marry someone with whom I would be more comfortable. His manner is most pleasing, and he is most truly the gentleman. I know that you wish me to be happy, and it seems to me that I would not be so with Mr. Westbrook. I regret that this did not seem apparent to me from the first, but I was so anxious to do what I thought to be the most prudent thing that I confess I did not allow myself to consider my own state of mind.*

She had gone on to say that she was writing to Mr. Westbrook by the same post, but that she would not share her decision with anyone until she knew that he and Mr. Westbrook had received the news.

To Mr. Westbrook, she had sent her deep regrets and her heartfelt thanks for the honor he had done her by asking for her hand. She assured him that she would always hold him in the highest esteem and that she trusted her decision would not cause him undue inconvenience, since it had been made so early in the engagement. She had sat for a moment, considering what his reaction might be to her letter, and she had finally decided that she must give him a reason of some sort. After thinking it over, she had added in her closing:

It does seem to me that, in time, each of us might well find another better suited in manner and disposition, and at that time regret that we had made our decision to wed in haste.

She did not allow herself to think of the fact that Mr. Westbrook had scarcely rushed to the altar, given his age, nor that such a comment could very well be interpreted to mean that she had already discovered such a one. She carefully avoided mention of James Gray.

The next morning she turned the letters over to Beavers, to be sent with the morning post, and, once again feeling that curious lightness of spirits that she had experienced yesterday, she went in to breakfast.

"Ah, here comes the blooming bride-to-be," said Nigel, holding up his cup in a mock toast. "You are again looking very well, Miss MacGregor."

"I wish that you would not talk about the wedding, Nigel," said Olivia. "It makes me out of reason cross, and I wish to enjoy myself today."

"Why does it make you cross?" demanded Nigel. "I

have been longing to know more about the gentleman in question."

"There is no need to discuss Mr. Westbrook," announced Elise. "We may do so at another time, but today I am once again bent upon enjoying the moment."

Ravinia nodded approvingly. "It is well to take advantage of the opportunity, my dear. As I told your father, I was sorry that you could not come to us for a Season. It would have done you great good to spend some time in London."

"That is very kind of you, Aunt," she replied. "Had our father not been so ill, I surely would have come. Now that he is doing somewhat better, Livy and I are delighted to be able to accept your hospitality."

"We go to the Belvederes' ball tonight," said Ravinia. "Have you something suitable to wear?"

Elise considered her wardrobe carefully. "I believe that I may, Aunt—although I am not certain it is modish enough for London."

"I shall send Dawson in to look at it," replied her aunt, referring to her own maid. "If it is not suitable, I am certain that Sally has something that she could lend you. We shall see both of you properly outfitted next week."

"May I go, too, Aunt?" asked Olivia eagerly.

"You are not yet out," pointed out Lucy quickly. "I scarcely think that such behavior would be acceptable."

Ravinia, who had been on the brink of saying the same thing herself, frowned at her daughter-in-law. Lucy had an unfortunate habit of assuming authority that was not her own, and the habit grated upon Ravinia's nerves.

"Come now, Mama. Never mind what Lucy says." Nigel knew his mother very well and took advantage of Lucy's misstep. "You know that company is thin during the holidays, and with this unholy fog, poor Muriel Belvedere will be fortunate if she has two dozen people tonight. It will scarcely be more than an at-home."

Olivia shot her cousin a grateful look and waited for her aunt's answer, wisely deciding not to press her own suit.

The matter was decided when Lucy pursed her lips and began, "Thin company or no, it still seems most unsuitable to me—"

"I shall decide what is unsuitable for my niece!" returned Ravinia briefly. She looked at Olivia, and a brief smile flitted across her face. "I suppose, miss, that I must have Dawson inspect your gown, too."

"Oh, thank you, Aunt!" exclaimed Olivia, jumping up from her chair to go round the table and kiss Ravinia on the cheek. "You are all kindness!"

Lucy sniffed loudly. "A young lady should conduct herself with a little more dignity," she observed. "I trust that you will be more circumspect in your behavior tonight."

Olivia looked at her sharply, but kept herself from replying. She was too happy to allow Lucy to disturb her mood. She returned to her place and finished her breakfast, whereupon she and Elise repaired to their chamber to inspect their gowns. They were soon joined by Dawson, whose critical eye missed nothing. What was well enough for the family or for a night at the theater with their cousins was one thing. Appropriate dress for a ball—even a small one, lightly attended—was another. Everything was subjected to the closest scrutiny.

Finally, Dawson was satisfied, and the young ladies sighed in relief. After nuncheon, Monty came to call, as did James Gray and Arthur Townsend. Since Ravinia had restricted the children to the schoolroom and nursery area for the afternoon, Nigel had remained home from the club, declaring that the weather was not fit for man nor beast.

"Shall we see you at the Belvedere affair tonight, Monty? Or are you fearful of driving out in the fog?" inquired Nigel of his brother, who had just finished a horrifying account of the dangers presented by the present weather. Percival Damon, a friend of his, had been set upon by footpads in the park and, according to Damon, had scarcely escaped with his phaeton and his life.

"Fearful?" exclaimed Monty indignantly. "Suppose you think I'm cow-hearted! I'm not such a paltry creature, but I don't wish to be set upon by footpads, either!"

"Well, you won't be driving in the park tonight, will you?" returned Nigel. "Why ever was Damon such a clodpole as to drive through the park in this fog?"

"His cattle needed exercise!" responded Monty, defending his friend. "Couldn't get it on the streets."

"He apparently didn't get it in the park, either—except when he endangered his horses by having them gallop when he couldn't see his hand ahead of his face," said Nigel unsympathetically. "Poor beasts are fortunate they didn't break a leg."

Monty glared at his brother, who remained unmoved.

"Well?" said Nigel.

"Well what?" demanded Monty.

"Are you going to be present at the Belvederes' ball tonight?" Nigel repeated patiently.

"Do come, Monty!" urged Olivia. "I'm to be allowed to attend, and I wish you to stand up with me so that I have at least one partner besides Nigel."

"Rest assured, Miss Olivia, that even if Monty should not come, you will have more than one partner. I hope to have the pleasure of dancing with you myself," said Arthur Townsend in his most gallant tone.

"Thank you, Mr. Townsend," replied Olivia in a dampened tone. Her excitement had run away with her, and she had forgotten what Townsend's response would undoubtedly be.

"And I would count myself most fortunate if both you, Miss Olivia, and you, Miss MacGregor, would stand up with me tonight," said James Gray, his eyes twinkling at the sight of Olivia's obvious distress at the thought of dancing with Townsend.

"Ah yes, Miss MacGregor—I do beg your pardon! Naturally, I also wish the honor of dancing with you tonight," added Townsend hastily, suddenly realizing his ungentlemanly omission.

"Thank you, Mr. Gray—and Mr. Townsend," she replied gravely, although her eyes were dancing as she glanced at James Gray. What a pleasure it was to be attended by a young man with a sense of humor, she told herself. He was so very different in every respect from Mr. Westbrook. Turning to Monty, she asked, "And will you come, too, Cousin?"

Monty nodded unhappily. "No choice. Must do the pretty, I suppose."

"Good man, Monty!" said his brother encouragingly. "Shall we call for you so that you don't have to brave it alone?"

Again Monty nodded unhappily, but Lucy, who, feeling that they needed a chaperon, had quietly joined them in the drawing room, demurred. "I don't know that there will be space enough for all of us, Nigel."

Monty stared at her, and Nigel inquired dryly, "Are you going then, Lucy?"

She nodded. "And Charles, of course, and Mama-in-law, and possibly Sally and Edward. It might be better, Monty, if you called for Nigel instead of our calling for you."

"Perhaps I could call for Nigel, as well as for Miss MacGregor and Miss Olivia, in my carriage—and then we could call for Monty," suggested James Gray. "My parents are gone from London, and I have the use of their vehicles."

"How delightful that would be!" exclaimed Olivia, smiling gratefully at him.

"I don't believe that would be at all suitable," Lucy began once more, but she was interrupted by Ravinia, who had slipped in unannounced and had been listening to the exchange.

"No, you are correct, Lucy," she said. But before Lucy could respond with more than a quick glow of pleasure at this endorsement, Ravinia continued, "You and Charles may take your carriage, Lucy. If Sally and Edward wish to attend, they may go with you or take their own vehicle. My nieces and Nigel will ride with me, and we will collect Monty on the way." She nodded briefly to James Gray and Arthur Townsend before leaving the drawing room. "We will look forward to seeing you there, gentlemen."

Lucy, severely annoyed by Ravinia's interference and her own inability to do anything about it, rose and nodded stiffly to the others before following her mother-in-law.

As the door closed behind her, Nigel drawled, "I wonder what terrible thing Charles did in a former life to find himself married to such a harridan?"

No one had any light to shed upon his question, so conversation returned once more to plans for the evening.

And the evening was everything—or almost everything—that Elise had hoped it would be. Their group was merry on the trip there, which, as Nigel pointed out, would not have been the case had Lucy been in attendance. The conversation was light, despite the weather, and one and all were prepared to enjoy themselves, even if the ball was scantily attended.

Elise and Olivia had been carefully inspected, first by Dawson and then by their aunt, and they were confident that they were dressed as young ladies of the *ton* should be. Both were attired in white crepe gowns over satin petticoats, the bodices and hems trimmed with satin ribbons and beads. Both wore pearl combs in their hair and pearl earbobs, both wore the pair of bangle bracelets presented by Monty over their long white gloves. They had been pronounced flawless by their inspectors, and Nigel and Monty had upheld the pronouncement.

Mrs. Belvedere was delighted to receive them for, as Nigel had predicted, her ball was anything but a crush. However, the orchestra played invitingly, the ballroom was charmingly decorated with potted palms and orange trees, and candlelight glowed on the well-polished floors. Monty offered Elise his arm, and Nigel led out Olivia as Ravinia watched approvingly.

"You have a handsome pair of sons, Ravinia," observed her hostess. She had no pressing need to remain at the door to greet her guests. Instead of a steady stream of arriving carriages that blocked the street, the arrivals were widely spaced, and she was free to mingle.

"Thank you, Muriel. They do well enough, I believe," replied Ravinia, who was well pleased with all her offspring. "And how are your children? Are they in attendance tonight?"

Muriel Belvedere, a plump woman with a motherly face and fading blue eyes, nodded. "There is Cecily in the blue gown," she replied, indicating a plump, pretty brunette on the arm of a tall, thin man, "with her husband, Davis St. James. And there is Belinda just behind them. She is recently engaged to James Kaufman."

Ravinia nodded. "I had read of their engagement in the paper. My congratulations, Muriel."

Mrs. Belvedere nodded. "Freddie and I were very pleased."

Ravinia glanced around the room. "But where is your son?" she inquired. "I thought that he was coming to stay with you during the holiday. Is he not in attendance tonight?"

Her hostess sighed in exasperation. "I have just sent

his father upstairs to tell him that he must come down to greet our guests. Walter is as he has always been—absorbed in his passion for the past and careless of his social obligations. We have very nearly given up the attempt to change him."

Ravinia nodded. "You have my sympathy, Muriel. It is a pity, for he is a fine-looking young man, and of course his intelligence is exceptional. I recall my son-in-law, Edward Godwin, speaking very highly of him when they were at university together."

"Intelligence is all very well in its place," responded Mrs. Belvedere, her normally pleasant expression creased with unhappiness, "but since he does not give a fig about anyone or anything save antiquity, it is not likely that he will ever have a normal life or a family of his own. The family line will stop with him."

At that moment, a young man in evening dress appeared in the entryway, his expression an unhappy blend of irritation and boredom.

"There he is, Ravinia. If you will excuse me, please." Mrs. Belvedere hurried over to capture her wayward son before he decided to bolt, and led him back to Ravinia.

"Walter, make your bow to Mrs. Longfellow." Turning to him as he made his perfunctory bow, she added, "You recall that her daughter Sally is married to Edward Godwin, whom you knew at university, dear."

"Of course," he said stiffly. "I hope they are well."

His tone indicated a considerable lack of interest in the subject, but Ravinia, keenly aware of his mother's distress at his manner, ignored it. "Indeed they are. As a matter of fact, they are here in London and will be here later this evening."

"That will be delightful!" exclaimed Mrs. Belvedere. There was a brief pause, then, glancing sharply at her son, she added, "Will it not be delightful, Walter?"

He had been staring across the room, but at her question he turned to look at her. "Did you say something, Mother?"

"I said, Walter, 'Will it not be delightful?'" she repeated patiently, speaking as one might to a particularly slow five-year-old.

He stared at her for a moment, his expression puzzled. "Will what be delightful, Mother?" he inquired. "You do need to explain yourself a little more clearly."

"Mrs. Longfellow has just said that Edward and his wife will be here later this evening," Mrs. Belvedere explained, remaining, Ravinia thought, remarkably calm under the circumstances. Her son's disregard for proper manners had grown greater year by year, and upon the few occasions he now appeared in society, his parents were unfailingly horrified by his conduct.

"Oh, indeed?" he responded, his brows lifted slightly. Ravinia nodded her affirmation, and both his gaze and his attention wandered away once more.

"Forgive us, Ravinia," his mother said in a low voice. Then, raising her voice once more to get his attention, she said, "Walter? I said, 'Won't that be delightful?' You should have responded that indeed it would be good to see Edward and his wife again."

He regarded her blankly for a moment, as though bringing his mind back from faraway places. Then, when he focused, he said, "But you have already said it, Mother. It would be redundant were I to echo you. Ma'am," he said, turning to Ravinia and bowing briefly before strolling away.

Mrs. Belvedere stared at her friend in despair. "Do you see what I mean, Ravinia? He never conducts himself as a gentleman should. He spends his time at his own home, studying everything he can discover about the ancient days of this country and traveling to inspect places where evidence of those days has been found. My husband cannot prevail upon him to go to the club or to go hunting with him, and he certainly would never attend a ball unless we held it at home. And, as you see, we have to beg him to do so even then." She sank wearily into a nearby chair. "I have very nearly given up hope."

Ravinia shook her head. "You should never do that, Muriel. He is a most unusual case, to be sure, but I daresay things will work out far better than you might expect."

"Do you think so?" asked the poor woman, brightening a little. "He is a kind enough man—just a very difficult, odd one."

Just then the butler appeared with another handful of guests, and she hastened over to make them welcome. Thoughtfully, Ravinia studied Walter Belvedere, who had made his way to a small bench, placed for privacy behind a group of potted palms. He sat there, appearing to regard the dancers with great seriousness, but Ravinia knew that his mind was far away. Without a question, civilizing Walter Belvedere presented a very interesting challenge. Ravinia enjoyed challenges, and she had always been very fond of Muriel Belvedere. It suddenly occurred to her that she might be able to help her unfortunate friend.

When she returned her full attention to the dancers, she saw that Elise was now dancing with James Gray and that Monty was with Olivia. She nodded thoughtfully when she saw her niece's bright expression as she looked up at her partner. A very taking young man, James Gray, she thought, and Elise appeared to agree with that assessment of him. Evan would probably not be pleased, but Ravinia considered her interest harmless enough. She did most certainly disapprove of marrying the girl off without a Season, nor so much as a look at the world. In Ravinia's opinion, having a little experience would help her take her place in society more gracefully—and more happily.

Elise was indeed delighted with her partner. He danced gracefully and his remarks were charming. Smiling down at her, he led her to the edge of the dance floor after finishing the set.

He excused himself to fetch refreshments for them, but before leaving, he bent close and said, "Pearls become you, Miss MacGregor. They emphasize the soft glow of your cheeks and your eyes."

So absorbed was Elise in what he had said and in admiring him as he walked down the room that at first she did not realize that anyone had spoken. She had thought she was alone, for the company was so thin that no one stood close by. Suddenly she was aware of a slight rustling in the palms behind her, and she moved to peer around them. To her surprise, there sat a young man who appeared to be glaring directly at her.

"I beg your pardon," said Elise doubtfully. "Did you say something to me just then?"

"I said, ma'am, 'What complete rubbish!'" he responded, his tone so remote that she still was unsure that he was speaking to her.

"What do you mean?" she asked. "*What* is complete rubbish?"

"What the young man was saying to you just then: 'They emphasize the soft glow of your cheeks and your eyes,'" he responded unexpectedly. "What a waste of a perfectly good evening that I could have spent in a worthwhile manner instead of watching a mating ritual and listening to such drivel!"

Elise, infuriated, drew herself up straight and glared at him. "You are offensive, sir!" she said in her iciest tone.

"No more so than you and your young man are to me!" he retorted.

Unable to think of an adequately crushing response, Elise turned and was about to march away, head held high, when she realized that her aunt was standing there. Ravinia had seen them become engaged in conversation, and decided that she would do her best to help Mrs. Belvedere with her backward son.

"I see that you have met Mr. Belvedere, Elise," said Ravinia.

"Mr. Belvedere?" she asked. "Do you mean that he is—"

"Mr. Walter Belvedere, the son of our hostess," her aunt inserted smoothly.

"Oh, that poor woman," said Elise, shaking her head.

Ravinia ignored her. "And this, Mr. Belvedere, is my niece, Miss Elise MacGregor."

"Probably better known as Pearl," remarked Mr. Belvedere, who appeared to be paying attention to the conversation, at least briefly. Ravinia could not follow what they were talking about, but this was the longest span of time she had seen Walter pay attention to a human being other than his mother in some time, and she felt that it was a hopeful sign.

The dancers were resuming their places on the floor, and Ravinia said quickly, "Elise, I should like for you to stand up with Mr. Belvedere for this dance."

Elise stared at her aunt in horror. "But Mr. Gray will be returning at any moment, and I had promised him—"

"Mr. Gray may have the next dance, Elise. After all, tonight we find ourselves in the unusual situation of having more gentlemen than we have ladies, so the gentlemen must take turns. Mr. Gray would not wish to be selfish."

Seeing that Walter Belvedere was still seated on the bench and showing no sign of moving, Ravinia bent down and took his wrist, raising him unwillingly to his feet. "Mr. Belvedere, it would make your mother very happy if you would dance. Perhaps if you would stand up just once, you would be allowed to retreat to your study once more without anyone bothering you."

His eyes, suddenly bright and alert, told her that she had gotten his attention, and a near smile fleeted across his lips. Then, bowing briefly to Elise, he offered his arm to lead her onto the floor. Elise looked beseechingly at her aunt, but then realized there was no help for it, and walked slowly onto the floor, her shoulders sagging slightly in defeat.

"Is your aunt always this aggressive?" Walter inquired. Elise nodded her head without speaking.

A long pause ensued, and when they were next standing close to one another, awaiting their part in the figure, he said, "She is at least a sensible woman."

"And am I to understand that I am not?" Elise snapped, her eyes sparkling in irritation.

He shrugged. "People who listen to rubbish gladly are seldom sensible."

Elise felt an almost irresistible urge to slap him; her fingers were fairly tingling with the desire to make sharp contact with the side of his smug, supercilious face. She was shocked by the violence of her feeling, for she prided herself on her calmness.

"Perhaps your definition of 'rubbish' wants refining," she replied smoothly, proud that she was able to hide her antipathy.

"Why?" he inquired carelessly. "It serves my purposes well enough. If I consider something to be rubbish, that is enough for me."

"Well, it is not enough for me!" she retorted, her voice rising slightly.

He looked at her in some surprise. "Why should it be? Why should you care what my definition is?"

She glared at him with such ferocity as they went through the steps of the figure that the young man with whom she next came face to face fairly flinched and searched his memory hastily to see if he had unwittingly offered her insult.

"You know very well why!" she hissed when they once again moved close to one another. "You were making light of a compliment you heard paid me in a private conversation."

"If you take it seriously, then that must be enough for you," he responded, his voice making it clear that he was completely uninterested in the topic. "Why should it matter to you that I or anyone else take it seriously?"

His complete lack of interest in either pursuing the discussion of his insult or in apologizing for it almost paralyzed Elise with anger. Had the punch bowl been within easy reach, she would have satisfied her fury by dumping it over his head. For a moment she indulged herself in the joy of imagining his expression. The young man standing next to her, who was still regarding her nervously, was badly shaken when she suddenly gave a brief, vicious laugh.

The most infuriating thing about the whole episode was the simple fact that he was correct—there was no reason she could think of why she should care whether he believed in the sincerity of Mr. Gray's compliment or not. By the time they reached the end of the dance, Elise was completely exhausted. She gave him a brief curtsy without glancing at him, turned on her heel, and walked away.

At the end of the room, Mrs. Belvedere was clutching her husband's arm. "Walter danced with someone, Freddie!" she exclaimed. "How perfectly wonderful!"

His father, exhausted by the effort of forcing Walter to attire himself appropriately and then dragging him downstairs, only shrugged. If one dance would please his wife, then he was happy. Balls were not his favorite activity, and he had a secret sense of fellow feeling with his son. He would much rather be elsewhere, too, and he watched with envy as Walter left the ballroom and took himself back to his study.

Elise's badly ruffled feelings were soothed in her next dance with James Gray. She had decided against sharing the insult delivered by Walter Belvedere. It would only make the rest of the evening unpleasant, and might even lead to Mr. Gray calling out Mr. Belvedere, something that she would never wish to have happen. Instead, she merely described briefly her aunt's interference and made light of the oddity of her partner.

"Yes, everyone knows how peculiar Walter Belvedere is," James Gray observed. "It's a pity. His parents are kind and his sisters are fine girls. I suppose every family has an odd one occasionally."

His observation comforted her, placing her tormentor safely among the odd ones, while they, of course, occupied the safer, more accepted ground.

"You were splendid to stand up with him," he said admiringly. "No one knows what to make of him."

"I didn't really have any choice," she reminded him. "Aunt Ravinia forced me into it."

"Still, you could have walked away from him—or, more likely yet, he could have walked away from you, as he has with others. You did extraordinarily well."

By the close of the evening, Elise felt exceedingly virtuous. They had a jolly ride home in the carriage, talking about the ball and gossiping about everyone.

"I saw you stand up with Walter Belvedere," commented Nigel curiously. "Edward was still at Oxford when Belvedere matriculated, and I understand he was something of a curiosity. We scarcely ever see him in town. What did he have to say?"

Elise shrugged lightly. "Nothing of consequence," she responded. "He *is* a peculiar sort, however."

Monty cleared his throat. "Know him myself—at least to bow to. Of course, he don't always recognize me."

"I don't think he recognizes anyone," said Nigel. "He appears to live in his own world."

Ravinia intervened. "He is merely quite different, I believe," she commented, putting a period to any further conversation about Walter Belvedere.

That night, Elise studied her reflection carefully in the glass, holding her pearl combs close to her hair and face.

"What are you doing?" Olivia asked her curiously.

"Do you think that the pearls cause my hair and eyes to glow, Livy?" she inquired seriously, peering into the glass.

Olivia patted her on the shoulder indulgently. "Of course they do, dear," she replied sleepily, and crawled into bed.

"Well, I think they must, too," Elise whispered defiantly to her reflection, then put the pearl combs away in a box. "No matter what some people say!"

Seven

"Hear about Prinny?" asked Monty, who had come to call despite the continuing heavy fog.

Elise and Olivia shook their heads, while Nigel merely raised an eyebrow.

"Tried to go to Hatfield to visit Lord Salisbury. Took them hours just to go a few miles and one of the outriders fell into a ditch. Finally had to give up and return to Carlton House."

"I can understand it," replied Elise, shivering slightly. "This dreadful fog is so thick that you could cut it with a knife."

Monty nodded several times. "Torches," he said.

"What about torches?" asked Nigel irritably.

"Using them. Saw a round dozen on my way over here," amplified Monty.

"Do you mean to say that they are using torches right now, in broad daylight, Monty?" cried Olivia.

Monty nodded again, then added, "Not broad daylight. Anything but."

The four of them went to the windows of the drawing room that looked out over the square. There was nothing to see except a wall of darkness.

"Not safe out. Don't recommend going out today, cousins," he advised. "Saw a coachman mistake the walkway for a road at one place. Ran over two men walking."

"How dreadful!" exclaimed Olivia.

"Dangerous," agreed Monty. "Walking their horses, most of them. Walked myself, on shank's mare. Couldn't risk my cattle in this."

"I have heard that even the mail coaches are having trouble getting through," commented Nigel. "The fog apparently doesn't lie just over London. They say it goes at least as far north as Birmingham."

Olivia looked at Elise. "I wonder if Papa will receive your letter any time soon or if it has been delayed by the weather."

"Likely delayed," observed Monty. "Glad it wasn't an important letter, matter of life and death."

Elise swallowed hard and managed a smile. "No, certainly not a matter of life and death."

Monty nodded, satisfied, and sat back comfortably until Nigel turned to him and remarked, "It seems to me from what you say, Monty, that you shouldn't venture back into the fog today."

Elise nodded seriously. "We wouldn't wish anything to happen to you, Monty, and it is truly too dreadful to go out again."

Olivia nodded in agreement, but Monty looked at them uneasily. "Do you mean stay here for the night?" he inquired. "No gear. Better to go home."

"Not at all!" protested Nigel. "You know that you can borrow anything you need from me or Charles or Edward. You must stay. We are concerned for your well-being, Monty."

A sudden pounding of feet on the stairway announced the approach of the children. Monty blanched and hurried toward the door nearest the entryway, but he wasn't quick enough. The horde poured in and surrounded him.

"No curricle!" he said quickly. "Fog! Foul weather!"

"Oh, that doesn't matter, Uncle Monty," Theodore told him. "Come and play draughts with us."

"Or Commerce," said Reginald, reaching in his pocket for a deck of cards.

Ravinia entered the room just then. "Monty, dear!" she exclaimed. "I'm so grateful that you are here! Now we will have the whole family safely together!"

"Just leaving," said Monty desperately, trying to make his way toward the door.

"Nonsense!" replied his mother. "You could have no engagements tonight, for everyone has been canceling because of the weather. You are much better off here with us."

Recognizing that he had been bested, Monty finally stopped struggling, and everyone settled down to entertain themselves until dinner. He, Reginald, and Theodore played a serious, cutthroat game of Commerce, with Niles and Nelson watching intently. Marjorie read a succession of stories to Tillie, and Bangs applied himself to gently gnawing the tassels of Monty's boots under the card table.

The parents had all taken advantage of the moment, happily abandoning their children to Monty while they pursued their own interests in other parts of the house. Charles and Edward were reading the newspaper and drinking brandy in the library, Sally was taking a nap, and Lucy was interfering with Cook in the kitchen, certain that she had a better recipe for preparing the burnt orange cream for dessert.

In the drawing room, Nigel was dozing gently by the fire, while Elise and Olivia were carefully perusing the latest copy of *La Belle Assemblée* and planning their new wardrobes. Ravinia stood by the window, apparently trying to peer through the opaque curtain of dark gray hung just outside.

"Is there anything wrong, Aunt?" inquired Elise, after watching her stand there for a quarter hour.

"No, of course not," Ravinia replied quickly. "It's just this dreadful weather. I suppose the best thing to do is to draw the curtains against it." So saying, she briskly set about shutting out the gloom, and the others were pleased by how effectively the gold velvet curtains cheered the room.

They had all just settled in comfortably once more when Beavers appeared in the doorway and cleared his throat to announce someone. All the ladies looked up expectantly, the two younger ones hoping that James Gray might, against all odds, have made his way there for the evening.

"Mr. Walter Belvedere has called, Mrs. Longfellow. Shall I show him in?"

"By all means, Beavers. Show him in immediately, and then bring him a glass of brandy against the cold."

"I am feeling a little chilly myself, Beavers," said Nigel, who had conveniently awakened at the mention of brandy. "Walter Belvedere?" he asked, turning toward Ravinia, his eyebrows raised. "Whatever can he want?"

"Hush, Nigel! Don't be an ungracious host," cautioned his mother, who had moved toward the door.

"Mr. Walter Belvedere," proclaimed Beavers, throwing open the door.

Belvedere entered, looking thoroughly chilled and thoroughly irritated. He was wearing quite a familiar expression, thought Elise. She might have felt some pity for him for being out in such weather if he had looked the slightest bit pleasant.

"Good evening, Mr. Belvedere," said her aunt graciously. "Won't you come over by the fire so that you may thaw from that ungodly cold?"

Belvedere accepted her invitation without comment, and stood with his back to the fire, staring at the other occupants of the room. Only Monty and the children and Bangs seemed unaware of his presence.

"I understand from my mother, ma'am, that you have in your possession a notebook in your library of considerable interest," he said to Ravinia.

Upon hearing this odd comment, Elise, Olivia, and Nigel turned to stare at her and were shocked to see that she nodded briskly.

"Yes, indeed," replied Ravinia. "I discovered it just recently in a box among my husband's things, and I thought that you might be interested in it. I, of course, know nothing of such things, although my husband's father was reckoned something of an expert about Roman Britain. This notebook is one that he kept of observations of various sites that he had visited and of items that had been found there."

"Naturally I am interested," said Belvedere abruptly. "May I see it?"

"Most certainly you may, sir—but after dinner. Do sit down and enjoy a brandy to warm your bones from this terrible cold. After dinner, I will take you to the library."

"I would prefer to go now," he responded shortly, turning from the fire and starting toward the door. Nigel and the others watched him in disbelief, and then looked at Ravinia to see if she were angered by her guest's abrupt behavior.

Amazingly enough, she looked perfectly calm. "I am certain that you would prefer to see it immediately, Mr. Belvedere," she replied gently, "but I would prefer that you see it after dinner."

She pulled the bell cord and Beavers promptly appeared. "Beavers, please tell Cook that there will be one more for dinner—and one more for breakfast tomorrow. And have the blue chamber prepared for tonight."

"Yes, Mrs. Longfellow," he responded, and silently withdrew.

Elise, Olivia, Nigel, and Walter Belvedere stared at her.

"If those preparations were for me, madam, you mistake the matter," said Belvedere, his teeth gritted. "I am remaining neither for dinner nor for the night."

Ravinia seated herself close to the fire and looked up calmly at her guest. "Very well, Mr. Belvedere. I regret that you have made such a long and unpleasant journey for nothing. Pray give your mother my best wishes. Beavers will bring you your coat, and I daresay we have an extra lantern you may take."

Here Ravinia rose once more and reached for the bell cord.

"Am I to understand, ma'am, that you will not allow me access to your library and the notebook you have spoken of unless I meet your terms?"

Ravinia smiled. "You have stated the matter very clearly, Mr. Belvedere."

He bowed to her briefly, acknowledging his defeat. "Then, by all means, I shall enjoy a brandy and go in to dinner with you and your family."

"I am delighted," responded Ravinia. "When we go in to dinner shortly, I would be obliged if you would escort my niece, Miss MacGregor. I believe that you have met."

Elise stared in horror first at her aunt and then at their guest.

A flicker of amusement crossed his face. "I believe that we have indeed met, Mrs. Longfellow. I shall look forward to being her partner for dinner."

Elise's moan was audible only to Olivia and Nigel. Olivia patted her hand encouragingly and Nigel whispered, "By God, I'll never get on Mama's bad side. If she can twist a care-for-nobody like Walter Belvedere around her little finger, there is no hope for the rest of us."

Eight

Dinner was an unusual experience. All of them, plus the children, with the charming addition of Walter Belvedere, sat down to the table together.

"Surely we will awaken soon and find that this has all been a nightmare," whispered Nigel to Olivia as he escorted her in. She nodded grimly, her eyes on her unfortunate sister. The meal itself was excellent, however, despite the company and despite Lucy's catalogue of criticisms about the various dishes.

"The buttered crab has too much sherry and too little anchovy paste," she complained. "And I believe that Cook forgot to put in the nutmeg." She paused to sample another dish, then added, "And the herrings most certainly are in need of more mustard butter."

"Lucy," said Ravinia, pausing a moment in her conversation with Edward.

"Yes, Mama-in-law?" she replied eagerly, hoping to hear a kindly comment about her astute observations.

"I forbid you to enter the kitchen again," said Ravinia shortly, turning back toward Edward.

"You forbid me to enter the kitchen?" responded Lucy blankly. "Whatever do you mean?"

Ravinia turned back to her, this time looking Lucy squarely in the eye, a look, as Nigel observed later, that would have turned a lesser mortal to stone. "I mean precisely what I said. You are not to enter my kitchen again or to counsel my cook—or, for that matter, any of my servants. I am in the habit of running my household as I see fit."

"Yes, of course you are, Mama-in-law, but I was only trying to—"

"Lucy," said Ravinia gently, "did you fail to understand some part of what I said?"

"No, but—" she began, staring at her mother-in-law.

"Then I would like to be able to continue my conversation with Edward, if I may do so," Ravinia said gently.

Lucy subsided into a pouting silence, and the others returned to their conversations, anxious to put the moment behind them.

"And so you have come to my aunt with an interest in a notebook," said Elise, trying desperately to think of something to say to her dinner partner.

Belvedere nodded briefly, and continued with his dinner.

"And you think that this notebook is something very interesting?" she prodded, staring at him. Drat the man! she thought. He was going to ignore every conversational gambit.

"I would scarcely have come out in such weather otherwise," he responded, glancing at her with disdain.

Irritation momentarily overcame her good manners. "Were you never told, Mr. Belvedere, that a gentleman makes polite conversation with his dinner partner?"

He glanced at her for a moment, then replied, "I believe I have heard my mother mention the matter." After another brief pause, he added, "Rubbish! A waste of time."

Elise bit her lip, but persisted. She would make at least one more attempt. He might be mannerless, but *she* knew very well how a well-bred individual was supposed to behave at dinner. Her heart went out to Mrs.

Belvedere for having to contend daily—or at least whenever he was in town—with such a boorish son.

"My aunt mentioned that her father-in-law was an expert about Roman Britain. I take it that you are also an expert."

To Elise's astonishment—and secret delight—Mr. Belvedere suddenly flushed and looked uncomfortable.

"No, I would not lay claim to being an expert—but I am most certainly very interested in the subject."

"Interested in England when the Romans lived here?" asked Monty in disbelief.

"Yes," Belvedere replied briefly. "I am interested in all parts of the ancient history of our country."

Monty stared at him, looking puzzled. "Why?" he asked.

"Why do you hunt, Longfellow? Or ride or drive your curricle about town?" returned Belvedere impatiently.

"Enjoy it," replied Monty.

"And that is precisely why I spend time studying ancient history."

Monty stared at Belvedere as though he were a lunatic who needed to be humored so that he would not lose control of himself and do damage to himself or others. "Read about it, do you?" he inquired with an air of spurious interest.

"Of course," said Belvedere, turning back to Elise to continue their conversation.

"I understand from your mother that you have established quite a library on the subject," said Ravinia, who had been following the discussion and was delighted to see that Belvedere had managed a conversation of reasonable length, even if it was not a particularly gracious one.

"Then I suppose that we will soon hear that you've become a member of the Roxburghe Club," remarked Nigel dryly.

"Roxburghe? The chap with all the books?" asked Monty.

Nigel appeared to have struck another area of interest, for Belvedere was the one to answer Monty's question. "Yes. The third duke was a bibliophile—"

"A what?" interrupted Monty, looking puzzled.

"A lover of books, Monty," said Nigel.

Walter Belvedere nodded and continued, "At any rate, after he died, his exceptional library was sold."

"Raised a little of the ready for the estate, did they?" inquired Monty sagely. He could well understand this interest in books if they brought in capital.

Belvedere smiled. "More than a little money, I'd say. The last of the books auctioned, a copy of Boccaccio's *The Decameron* that was printed in 1471, sold for more than two thousand pounds."

Monty's fork very nearly missed his mouth. "Two thousand pounds for a book!" he exclaimed, his eyes wide with disbelief.

Belvedere nodded, his eyes bright. "It was a very rare edition."

"Should hope so!" murmured Monty. "Two thousand pounds for a book!" It took him a moment to recover, but then he asked, "So what is this Roxburghe Club?"

"At the time of the sale of the library, a group of bibliophiles, led by Lord Spencer, had dinner together and began the club," replied Belvedere.

"Sit around and read, do they?" inquired Monty doubtfully.

"I believe they do rather more eating of fine food and drinking of fine wine," observed Nigel.

"They are also most interested in preserving rare books," responded Belvedere.

"Want to be a member, do you?" asked Monty, remembering his brother's earlier comment.

"Too elite for me," said Belvedere, shaking his head.

"I am most certainly interested in rare books, particularly those pertaining to history, but most of the gentlemen who are members have private libraries with significant holdings of rare books far larger than mine." Here he laughed briefly. "I am a student of such things, but I am scarcely in a position to own them."

"I cannot see that it matters particularly whether you are a member of that group or not, Mr. Belvedere," said Ravinia, who had been listening carefully to her guest. "What does matter is that you, like my brother Evan, are interested in such things and wish to see them preserved."

He nodded. "And I am most certainly interested, ma'am—just as I am interested in antiquity. I would be grateful if you would show me to your library so that I may see the notebook you have spoken of."

"And so I shall, sir—after we have dined," Ravinia replied. "The notebook—actually it is more of a sketchbook with extensive notes—records my father-in-law's journeys to quite a variety of sites."

"Indeed?" he asked, his eyes bright with interest. "And were his journeys limited to the south of England, or did he travel farther afield?"

"I have read only a few of his notes since finding it, but it appears to me that he traveled the length and breadth of Britain, looking at the remains of villas and forts and spas and potteries—anything he could find that was evidence of what life was like during that time. He was apparently inspired by seeing Greek and Italian remains while on the Grand Tour."

At this point, she stood and led the ladies and children to the drawing room. Mr. Belvedere started to rise as well, but Ravinia smiled at him and said, "Do remain with the gentlemen and have your port, sir. There will be time enough for the notebook later this evening."

Nigel and Monty glanced at each other, knowing

themselves to be cornered. "Never so grateful to have Charles and Edward by me in my life," remarked Monty to Elise later. "Not much of a fellow for books or old things myself, so wouldn't have had a notion of what to say to Belvedere."

Elise had enjoyed dinner far more than she had expected. Mr. Belvedere's strong interest in the past, so much like her father's, had surprised her, and she had appreciated her aunt's masterly manipulation of him. It still seemed a very odd time for him to come in search of the notebook—but then, Mr. Belvedere was undeniably a very odd man.

Marjorie had seated herself at the pianoforte, still playing carols for the pleasure of herself and the other children. Tillie and Bangs sat close to her, watching her playing carefully. Marjorie was a very pleasant child, Elise had decided, very unlike her mother in temperament. Lucy was at that moment busily reprimanding the twins for being too noisy, and Sally, who had just entered the room, was bearing down upon her sister-in-law.

"I do hope that the gentlemen hurry, or that Aunt will not be long," sighed Olivia. Ravinia had excused herself to attend to a problem elsewhere. "Perhaps we will be spared some of this brangling." The strain of having two families of children under one roof was beginning to tell. Sally and Lucy could scarcely be in the same room together for five minutes before problems began.

To their relief, Ravinia reappeared almost instantly, and the gentlemen did not linger at the table that evening.

"Scarcely got a sip of my port," complained Monty in a low voice as he seated himself next to Elise. "Belvedere fairly rushed us out of there."

He paused a moment, then grinned. "Not such a bad thing, really. Saved me from having to talk about the Romans."

Belvedere made his way directly to Ravinia as soon as he had entered the room. Curious to hear the exchange between them, Elise stood up and moved to stand before the fireplace, where she could hear their conversation without appearing to eavesdrop.

"Will you show me to the library now, ma'am?" he inquired briskly.

To Elise's amusement, her aunt replied, "A little later, Mr. Belvedere. I should like for you to spend some time with my family first."

Belvedere stared at her in disbelief. "I have just spent the past two hours with your family, Mrs. Longfellow," he pointed out reasonably, if not graciously. "And why the devil would you wish for me spend even five minutes with them?"

It was a reasonable question, Elise reflected, and she awaited the answer with interest. However, before he could reply, a conflict between Nelson and Niles broke out, and the air was thick with wailing and warning barks from Bangs.

"They have been kept up too late," remarked Sally apologetically. "They should have taken their supper in the nursery tonight."

The younger children departed in a flurry of boots and barking, and Belvedere watched with raised eyebrows.

"Is this what you meant when you said that you wished me to spend more time with your family?" he inquired of Ravinia.

She shook her head, her expression rueful. "As you can see, sir, we have been too much together. This is a large house, but this dreadful weather has kept everyone in so closely that I fear our nerves are giving way. It is good for us to have someone new here for the evening. You bring us a breath of fresh air."

Elise smiled to herself at his expression. Undoubtedly

this was the first time that anyone had told Walter Belvedere that he was a beneficial social influence.

"Now," said Ravinia, "I know that Edward has been looking forward for a chance to chat with you, and I am certain that he had no opportunity to do so at the end of dinner, since the other gentlemen were present." And here she firmly propelled him to the chair next to Edward's.

To Elise's surprise, Mr. Belvedere and Edward did apparently strike up a conversation of sorts. She did not really know Sally's husband very well, but she was aware that his interests were a little more scholarly than those of the rest of the family. At any rate, Mr. Belvedere apparently managed to maintain a conversation during the time that it took Monty and the two boys to complete three rousing hands of Commerce. At that point Ravinia took pity upon her guest and guided him to the library.

"Do make yourself comfortable, Mr. Belvedere," she told him, placing the box that contained the pages of the notebook and what was left of its leather binding on the table in front of him. "You will find writing materials should you wish to take notes of your own. Ring for Beavers if you require anything, or if you have any questions, by all means seek me out in the drawing room."

"Thank you, Mrs. Longfellow," he said stiffly, obviously eager to get to the manuscript, but aware that she had provided the opportunity to see it. "I would be grateful if you would tell me when you are retiring so that I may take my leave then."

"Take your leave?" she said, frowning slightly. "Do you mean to say that you are thinking of going back out in this weather?"

He nodded. "Naturally I will return home tonight—and, with your permission, I shall come again tomorrow to continue my reading. I know that you would not wish the notebook to leave your home."

"You may read all night if you wish to do so, Mr. Belvedere, but Beavers has prepared a chamber for you. By no means do I wish you to go back out into this fog, particularly late at night. It is too dangerous."

Belvedere, whose eyes had brightened at the mention of reading all night, bowed. "Very well, ma'am. I accept your hospitality with gratitude."

"Very pretty, Mr. Belvedere," Ravinia responded, smiling slightly. "With time you may have very passable manners."

He looked mildly surprised at her words, but his attention was already directed toward the notebook, and she closed the door carefully behind her as she left. He had already made great progress, she thought to herself with satisfaction. When she had suggested her idea to Muriel Belvedere, the poor woman had been so overcome with gratitude that she had wept. Using the notebook as bait to tempt him into social situations that he normally avoided like the plague was working very well—and it was satisfying that someone outside the family was reading the notebook. All in all, Ravinia was very pleased with herself.

When she returned to the drawing room, Nigel rose and closed the door behind her, then said, "Mama, whatever is Walter Belvedere doing here?"

She looked at him in surprise. "Why, you know what he's doing here, Nigel. He is reading your grandfather's notebook that I mentioned."

"But why is he reading it now—today?"

"Apparently because I told his mother about it last night and she mentioned it to him."

"And so he rushed right over here in this hideous fog to read a notebook that my grandfather kept sixty years ago?" demanded Nigel in disbelief.

"Well, you can see for yourself, Nigel, that he is quite passionately interested in it, just as your grandfather was," Ravinia pointed out. "I don't find his behavior surprising."

"But how will he get home tonight?" asked Elise. "He cannot go back out, can he?"

Ravinia shook her head firmly. "Of course not. He will spend the night here."

"Here? That is all we need, one more member for our happy band!" exclaimed Nigel, moving toward one of the windows. "Let me just have a look outside. Perhaps the weather is improving."

Monty beat him there and pulled back one of the curtains to peer out. He shook his head. "Out of luck, Nigel," he said. "Snow."

The others moved to the window and saw that Monty was not mistaken. Snow was falling thickly, already blowing in small drifts upon the window ledge.

"Well," said Nigel, turning back to the others, "it appears that we will all have the opportunity to get to know Mr. Belvedere much better."

Nine

The next morning the snow was still falling heavily, and a north wind rattled the windowpanes as Elise and Olivia pulled out kerseymere gowns and shawls to keep themselves warm. They dressed as quickly as they could in front of the fire.

"If I had a toasting fork, I'd put my slippers on it and warm them," Olivia moaned. "They are as cold as though they had been left outside in the storm. If Mary hadn't brought up the water just this morning, it would be frozen in the pitcher and we wouldn't be able to wash."

"Now we must go down to breakfast," grumbled Elise, "and I suppose Mr. Belvedere will be there. Why must the man be here for a snowstorm so that he can't go away again? He doesn't even like us."

"Ah, but he likes the notebook, dear sister," said Olivia, grinning. "And I noticed that he actually said more than three words to you at dinner yesterday evening. Perhaps he likes you as well. Now that you have met someone so utterly charming, perhaps you shall be moved to renounce Mr. Westbrook."

Elise, grateful that Olivia didn't know how close to the truth she was, flung one of her slippers at Livy, who ducked happily. At least no one, except perhaps Nigel, suspected her feeling for James Gray—and certainly no one yet knew that she had cried off from her engagement. She was determined not to think more about that until she had heard from her father. For the moment, she would enjoy herself.

"Well, you must admit that having Mr. Gray here instead of Mr. Belvedere would be a great improvement," said Elise. "But I suppose you would prefer the company of Mr. Townsend."

It was Livy's turn to send one of her own icy slippers flying at her sister, and afterward it took some moments to rearrange their clothing and to smooth their hair into place. Then, linking arms, they made their way down to the dining room, where Monty was morosely drinking coffee and eating a beefsteak.

"What's wrong, Monty? Worried about your cattle in all this snow?" asked Olivia, seeing his expression. Monty normally did not become unduly distressed about too many things other than his curricle and his horses.

He shook his head. "Belvedere," he replied. "Mama's gone to drag him from the library to take his breakfast with us. Been there all night."

"Mr. Belvedere has been in the library all *night?*" demanded Olivia. "He has been in there reading that notebook all this time?"

Monty nodded. "Likely going to tell us all about it," he said, more mournfully still.

"How could he have sat up all night poring over some ancient notebook?" commented Olivia, helping herself to tea from the silver urn on the sideboard and to plum cake and toast. "I should have gone sound asleep in less than ten minutes."

Monty nodded vigorously, relieved that someone else felt as he did. "Stretched out on the carpet in front of the fire," he agreed, addressing himself to his beefsteak with more enthusiasm. "Likely that's what he did if he's a sensible man."

Feeling more cheerful than he had since his mother's

ominous departure for the depths of the library, he regarded his cousins with a kindly eye, taking in their
attire.

"Those gowns all the rage in the country?" he inquired gently. Monty had a very nice eye for fashion, and
he felt it his duty to guide his relations when necessary.
Their kerseymere gowns were plainly made and their
single purpose was to provide warmth.

"No, Monty, they are not considered modish anywhere—and you needn't worry," replied Elise. "We
chose these to keep out the cold. We have no intention
of wearing them out where anyone will see us."

Thus reassured, Monty sat back easily in his chair, sipping his coffee. He was comforted to know that he would
not be alone to bear the burden of Belvedere's presence.
Nigel entered a minute later, just as Ravinia returned with
Walter Belvedere in tow. Monty and the young ladies inspected Belvedere with interest, certain that they would
see eyes bloodshot from reading and clothing wrinkled
from sleeping on the carpet or the sofa. They were disappointed to see no such signs of an uncomfortable night.
Mr. Belvedere looked bright-eyed and neatly attired; he
did, in fact, look to be in better condition than Nigel, who
appeared far from rested and whose neckcloth had been
hurriedly arranged with fingers stiff from the cold. Normally impeccably groomed, Nigel was irritated by the
knowledge that today he and his valet had fallen far short
of their usual perfection.

"I say—" began Monty, as Nigel eased himself into the
chair farthest from the windows and closest to the fire.

"If you are about to say anything about my cravat,
Monty, I would recommend that you reconsider," inter-
rupted Nigel, giving his attention to his warm cup of tea.
"I wish you good morning, ladies," he said, nodding to
Elise, Olivia, and his mother. "Mr. Belvedere," he added,
nodding to that gentleman.

Nigel paused when he focused upon Belvedere. "You are looking very well, sir. Unusually so. The cold must agree with you."

"I believe that it is the notebook, not the cold, that has had such a salutary effect upon Mr. Belvedere. He has been reading it all night, have you not, sir?" inquired Elise.

"All night?" exclaimed Nigel. "Without sleep?"

"All night," confirmed Mr. Belvedere briskly. "Without sleep."

"You must be mad," observed Nigel flatly, just as he might have said, "You have a new hat."

"It is possible," conceded Belvedere. "It is, after all, a mad world in which we live."

"And a philosopher as well!" groaned Nigel, crouching closer to the rapidly fading warmth of his cup of tea.

"You are hardly being a gracious host, Nigel!" observed his mother tartly.

Nigel regarded her closely for a moment, then nodded in agreement. "As usual, you are absolutely correct, Mama. My apologies, Belvedere," he said, bobbing his head briefly in that gentleman's direction in the semblance of a bow. "I fear that I am out of sorts because I am still half frozen from the night. I was not meant for weather such as this. I am thinking of taking ship for the West Indies as soon as it is possible to travel."

Monty regarded him with some concern. "Yellow fever," he said briefly. "Wouldn't go there if I was you. Not healthy."

"I don't think that Nigel is really thinking of going there, Monty," said Elise soothingly. "I believe he is just wishing for warm weather."

Monty nodded. "Very sensible not to go. Heard of three fellows who died there. Better to be cold here than dead there."

"Well, now I am comforted," said Nigel, "knowing that

I have made the correct decision. I can only pray that I will not be found dead of the cold here."

Walter Belvedere had been following this exchange with the trace of a smile, and Ravinia had observed it. Pleased to see even this glimmer of warmth, she attempted to draw him in to the conversation.

"Mr. Belvedere, do tell us what you found in the notebook that was interesting enough to keep you awake all night."

Monty cringed visibly when she said this, and even went so far as to shake his head slightly, but he quickly regained control of himself and, conscious of his manners, attempted to appear interested. Belvedere had missed none of this, and his smile grew slightly.

He shook his head. "There is no reason to trouble the others with this matter, Mrs. Longfellow. The interest is mine, not theirs."

The others were relaxing and beginning to look upon Belvedere more kindly when Ravinia replied, "Nonsense! Of course we wish to hear about it!"

"Wouldn't press him, Mama," urged Monty. "Not the polite thing to do."

Belvedere, unable to resist the temptation, rose from the table and said, "Perhaps you would all like to come to the library with me. I will deliver a brief lecture on what I have discovered—it will take no more than an hour or so—and then I will read aloud some of the more significant passages and my notes about them."

There was a moment of tense silence until Belvedere smiled and said gently, "What? No takers? You shock me," and seated himself once more as the others gave way to reluctant laughter.

"Very clever," said Nigel. "You had us believing you." Monty, who had blanched visibly, nodded in agreement.

"Oh, I meant it," replied Belvedere. "I will be available—apparently for the remainder of the day and evening," he said, glancing at the whistling whiteness outside the window, "for any of you who wish to see the notebook."

Ravinia did not press the matter, pleased with what had been accomplished thus far. Walter Belvedere could be a perfectly acceptable young man—eccentric, of course, but there were many in their society who prided themselves on their eccentricity—if only he could remove the chip from his shoulder.

The others were still idling over their breakfasts when he excused himself and returned to the library.

"Decent chap," observed Monty, after the door had closed behind him. "Wouldn't have thought it."

There was a murmur of agreement and then a few idle suggestions about how to pass the day.

"I have some letters to write," said Ravinia. "I may as well do that, since there'll be no going out today."

The others were strongly in favor of a game of whist, so they drew the card table close to the fire in the drawing room and made themselves comfortable.

"Children are staying up in the nursery, Charles?" inquired Monty, gazing nervously at the door.

Charles nodded. "You're quite safe for an hour or two, Monty. Lucy has decided that they should have a few lessons while they're here, so she's marched them off to the old schoolroom, and Sally is playing games with hers in the nursery."

Monty relaxed and settled in for serious concentration.

"Charles, would you not like to play?" inquired Elise.

"I wouldn't mind," he replied, "but you've already got four."

"Here. You come and partner Monty," she said, standing up. "I have the headache, and I believe I'll lie down until it clears."

"May I bring you something?" asked Livy in concern.

Elise smiled. "No, I'll be fine," she said. "Just a little rest should do the trick."

Before she went upstairs to her chamber, however, curiosity got the better of her, and she slipped quietly into the library. Mr. Belvedere was bent over the notebook, so intent upon what he was studying that he did not hear her approach.

She cleared her throat slightly, but he didn't look up.

"Good morning again, Mr. Belvedere," she said cheerfully, hoping that that would attract his attention.

It apparently did not, for his head remained bowed over his work. Coming closer, she moved to his side so that she could see what he was studying so intently. So far as she could tell, there was a sketch of a woman's face, with extensive notes made in black ink down the side of the page.

"Who is she?" asked Elise, not really expecting to receive an answer. "A goddess?" This was a reasonable question, she felt, for on the page facing this one was a sketch of a woman's face, only it was obviously of Minerva.

"No," replied Belvedere, finally looking up at her. "And that is the extraordinary thing! So many of the mosaics *do* picture the gods, but this one appears to be the face of a young girl of the family. The craftsman must have made the floor especially in her honor."

"She's very pretty," observed Elise, trying to think of something to say.

Mr. Belvedere snorted. "I suppose that *would* be the first thing you would think of," he replied.

Elise colored. "You do realize, do you not, Mr. Belvedere, that it is possible to speak to another human being without insulting her?"

He shrugged. "I suppose it is possible, but it is not in my nature to hide my feelings. I am honest and must speak my mind."

"Indeed?" she inquired icily. "I should not call that honesty so much as lack of control."

He glanced at her in surprise and appeared to consider her comment for a moment. "Possibly so," he conceded. "Still, I must say what I think."

"What do *you* think is important about this mosaic, aside from its beauty?" she asked.

"Just what I said," he replied. "The subjects were normally related to the gods." Here he turned back several pages and pointed to a sketch that pictured Orpheus and Eurydice, then to one that showed Minerva, Venus, and Juno with Paris and the golden apple.

"These were the normal subjects," he continued, "but obviously some of the artists were beginning to make their art more personal."

"Or the owner of the villa who was paying him commissioned this one," she remarked.

"It could be so, but Mr. Longfellow appears to have found several, judging by his sketches and notes."

"What else have you discovered that made you interested enough to sit up all night poring over this?" she asked curiously.

He picked up a sheet of his notes and held it toward her. "Here," he said, pointing to a sketch of three rings. "These might interest you." He pointed to one, a graceful ring that he said had been made of gold. "It was for a young girl named Aemilia. You can see her name in the open work."

She pointed to one that showed a pair of clasped hands. "What about this one?" she asked.

"Probably a betrothal ring," he said, "thus the clasped hands. And this one was also for a lady."

"How can you tell?" she asked. "Does it also say her name?"

He shook his head. "Longfellow's notes say that it is inscribed as the 'love charm of Lucius'—and considering how handsome a ring it is, and how greedy most people are for pretty things, I should imagine that Lucius was quite successful with his charm."

"And are you not greedy for pretty things yourself, Mr. Belvedere?" she asked. "Are you not the one who is sketching these lovely rings so that you have a record of them for yourself?"

He flushed a little. "I don't wish to own them," he said abruptly. "Merely to record and study them."

"I see. That, of course, is quite a different matter," she said, her tone indicating that it was not at all a different matter. She thought a moment of her father and the album he kept of his findings. It was possible, she knew, to be interested in such things without behaving as Mr. Belvedere did. She considered mentioning her father's interest to him, but decided that she really wanted no more conversation with the man than was necessary.

She rose and walked toward the library door. "I shall leave you to your reading and note taking, Mr. Belvedere."

There was silence behind her, and she turned to see if she had distressed him.

Walter Belvedere was bent once more over his work, clearly unaware of whether she was in the room or out of it.

Elise shook her head and closed the door silently behind her.

Ten

Elise's attempts to take a nap proved ineffectual. She took a headache powder, lay down upon her bed, and suddenly discovered that the only thing she could hear was the wind and the sweep of the snow. She was cold and out of sorts—and half fearful that she had done a most foolish thing by writing to Mr. Westbrook. She still knew that she did not particularly wish to marry him; she would much prefer to marry someone like—well, someone like Mr. Gray. She would be far happier, she was certain, for he had a happier, kinder manner than did Mr. Westbrook, and he was, of course, much younger, too. Still, Mr. Gray had not asked to marry her, and Mr. Westbrook, a well-respected and wealthy gentleman, had. Nonetheless, she thought, the die had been cast when she sent the letter. If she had been foolish—and she was quite certain she had been—then she would simply have to live with the consequences.

Besides, she told herself, as she combed her hair and freshened her gown to go back downstairs, Mr. Gray had been very attentive. She should not repine, for who knew what the future would bring? If the weather had been good, she and Olivia would have been too busy for her to fall into a fit of the dismals. Pinching her cheeks to restore a little color and forcing herself to look cheerful, she went back to the drawing room to join the rest of the family.

She was amused to discover that the original game of whist had been overset by the demands of the children, who had borne Monty off in triumph to the billiards room. The table was now occupied by Olivia, Nigel, Sally, and Charles, with Lucy standing first behind Charles, then behind Sally. Olivia and Nigel both held their cards close to their chests whenever she moved in their direction, Nigel eying her with irritation. Ravinia was nowhere to be seen.

"Lucy, *do* please sit down," said Sally. "It makes me a nervous wreck to have you peering over my shoulder all the time. If you want to take my hand, I will give it to you."

"No, you won't, Sally," said Charles, before Lucy had an opportunity to reply. "I'm not going to partner with Lucy. She has an abysmal lack of card sense."

"Charles, you know that's not true!" replied Lucy, offended. "Why, Teresa Stillwell and I always win at whist!"

"Naturally," he responded without looking up from his cards. "Teresa wins no matter who she plays with."

"Well, I do think you should permit me to play. Everyone else has had the opportunity," replied Lucy petulantly.

"Then you may play my hand," said Charles shortly, preparing to rise from his chair when he encountered the outraged expressions of the other three players and the toe of Sally's slipper against his shin.

"Upon second thought, my dear, here's another deck. Why don't you play patience until we've finished?"

Elise stood perfectly still in the doorway until Lucy had laid out the cards for patience and reluctantly begun her game. She had not the least desire to be cornered to play any game with Lucy, who would probably wish to do something delightful if she spotted Elise, like spending the rest of the afternoon playing cribbage. Carefully she crept back out into the passageway to avoid detection.

She stood there for a moment, considering the prob-

lem. She did not wish to go back to her room or to join
Monty in the billiards room. A quick reconnaissance re-
vealed that neither the smaller drawing room nor the
morning room had a fire, probably to conserve coal
since so many of the bedchambers were in use and required heat. It seemed doubtful that any more fuel
could be delivered for some time, given the state of the
weather.

Elise sighed. She did not wish to seek out Ravinia, nor
did she feel that she could take herself off to the kitchen,
which would undoubtedly be warm and bustling with activity. There was really no other choice.

She returned to the library.

She opened the door gently and saw that Mr. Belvedere was still bending over his work, which was naturally
not a surprise. But the fire was glowing comfortably, so
she pulled a book from a nearby shelf and settled herself
quietly in a chair close by its warmth. All was peaceful,
the only sounds the scratching of Mr. Belvedere's pen
against the paper and the occasional turning of a page,
and her eyes slowly closed.

"Well, isn't this a cozy scene?"

Elise heard Nigel's familiar voice as though from a
great distance. Finally she managed to lift her heavy lids
and look at him.

"Good afternoon, Nigel," she murmured, stretching.

"Good evening would be more accurate, cousin," he
informed her. "Dinner is about to be served, and you
were nowhere to be found. Olivia went up to your chamber to wake you, and when you were not there, she
became very upset. I believe she thought that you had
wandered out into the blizzard to go to sleep and had
quietly frozen to death."

Elise smiled. "Livy has a fine sense of drama," she told
him.

"Yes, I have indeed noticed that," he informed her.

"She wanted us to call out the dogs for a search party, but I told her that all I had to offer was myself—and Bangs, of course, but I believe he is still helping Monty play billiards."

At that, Elise's eyes finally opened fully. "Monty is still with the children?" she demanded.

Nigel nodded. "I believe that he feels he has discovered an extraordinary talent in Theodore and has appointed himself his mentor. If he is as good as Monty says he is, I daresay Theo will make enough money from wagering on his prowess at billiards to set himself up for life."

Here he turned toward Mr. Belvedere, whose presence Elise had forgotten about completely.

"I trust that my cousin has not disturbed you too much, Belvedere. I fear that she probably snores."

"Nigel!" exclaimed Elise. "That is scarcely a polite observation—and it is most untrue, too!"

Mr. Belvedere still had not looked up, his pen continuing to move across the paper, but he said without a glance, "In reality, Miss MacGregor, I believe that it would be more accurate to say that you gurgle."

"Gurgle?" she gasped.

He nodded, still not looking up. "A very interesting sound, actually. It begins as a snore, but changes abruptly to a sort of bubbling sound."

"How very musical of you, Elise," said Nigel. "Even in your sleep you are performing. I would have thought it of Olivia, but then you *are*, after all, the singer."

"What Mr. Belvedere says is rubbish," she replied, savoring the word "rubbish" as she said it. "He is simply trying to annoy me since I annoyed him by invading his privacy for my nap."

At this point, Olivia and her aunt entered the library. Olivia rushed over to Elise and threw her arms about her sister.

"Are you quite all right?" she demanded. "I was distraught when I could not find you, Elise! I felt like the greatest beast in nature because I didn't go up to check on you earlier when I knew you weren't feeling well."

"Don't fly up into the boughs, Livy. I am perfectly well. In fact, my nap here by the fire has quite restored me." She gave Olivia a reassuring hug.

"And," added Nigel, "I have discovered that Elise does not snore. She gurgles while she is sleeping."

Olivia giggled. "That is a very apt way to describe it, Nigel. Isn't it the oddest sound?"

"I am not the one who heard it or described it," returned Nigel. "Mr. Belvedere must take the credit on both counts."

"I do *not* snore, Livy!" protested Elise, horrified by the turn the conversation had taken.

"No," replied Nigel gravely, "you gurgle, Elise, which is a much different matter. You must not let it prey upon your mind."

"Come now, Elise," said her sister, taking her hand and pulling her up from her chair. "It is very nearly time for dinner. Aunt Ravinia said we are not to change because it is too cold to wear anything other than our warmest clothes."

The three of them had started toward the door when Elise said reluctantly, "Don't you wish to come in to dinner, Mr. Belvedere?"

Mr. Belvedere glanced up and briefly shook his head, then returned immediately to his work. Nigel lifted his eyebrows and shrugged his shoulders in silent comment to his cousins, and they turned once more to leave.

"Nonsense, Mr. Belvedere! Of course you will come in to dinner," said Ravinia, who had been listening to the exchange from the doorway. "You have been working in here all day and it is more than time to come out with the rest of us for a bit."

"I am not hungry, ma'am," he replied. "I have very nearly gotten through the notebook once, and I would prefer to continue."

"You are going to have an adequate amount of time to go through it more than once more," Ravinia said. "The snow is showing no sign of stopping, and the wind has not ceased to blow. Nothing is moving on the streets, so you will be spending the night with us once more."

She paused, but he did not respond immediately, instead continuing to write as though he was fearful that he would forget his thoughts on the subject if he did not commit them to paper immediately.

"I would remind you, sir, that I have not finished going through the trunk in which I found the notebook you are presently reading. Should I discover anything else, I would assume that you would wish to see it."

Here he did look up. "Yes, of course I would, Mrs. Longfellow."

She smiled gently. "If that is the case, Mr. Belvedere, I shall look forward to seeing you in the drawing room in a very short space of time." And she turned and left the room.

"Best come if you want to see whatever else she finds, Belvedere," Nigel advised. "I tell you on the best of authority that she means what she says."

And so it was that Elise found herself once again escorted in to dinner by Walter Belvedere. Although this was still far from what she wanted to be doing, tonight she found that she could at least tolerate the situation. It was a case, she thought, of knowing what to expect. Too, she found herself feeling rather sorry for Walter Belvedere, despite his brusque manner. The fact that he was interested in the rings that he had copied the sketches of and in the face of the young girl in the mosaic made her feel that he might be slightly more human than she had thought him. Of course, he still thought very poorly of her and what he perceived as her tendency to enjoy pretty things, and he had told Nigel and Olivia that she gurgled in her sleep, but she still felt slightly more comfortable with him than she had on the previous night.

Of course, that was before dinner. Dinner itself was another matter.

"I propose that we go for a brisk walk around the square after dinner," said Nigel, as they seated themselves for the first course.

Monty, who was sometimes inclined to be painfully literal, stared at his brother. "Snow," he said. "Can't even see the square, Nigel. Likely to die in a drift."

"A very reasonable thought, Monty. I find myself persuaded," he replied, lifting his glass in a toast to his brother. "We will remain indoors."

Lucy rolled her eyes. "And I suppose the two of you think that is amusing," she said. "I would wish for our dinner conversation to have a little higher tone, if only because the children are here."

"But we like it, Mama," said Theodore. "It *is* amusing." And Reginald nodded his agreement. The younger ones were more deeply absorbed in their dinner, and Marjorie was helping Tillie to smuggle the choicest tidbits from her plate to the anxiously waiting Bangs.

Theodore's self-confidence had grown by leaps and bounds during the day spent in the billiards room. He had been transformed from the second-born son to a young man with the golden touch. He had seen how impressed Monty was with his talents and, since he was equally impressed with Monty's talent with the ribbons, Theodore saw himself in an entirely new light. Up until now, he had followed Reginald's lead. When Reginald had told him to place rocks in the pockets of his jacket and then to pitch them at the pieman, he had done as he was told—just as he always had. He had always obeyed Reginald, occasion-

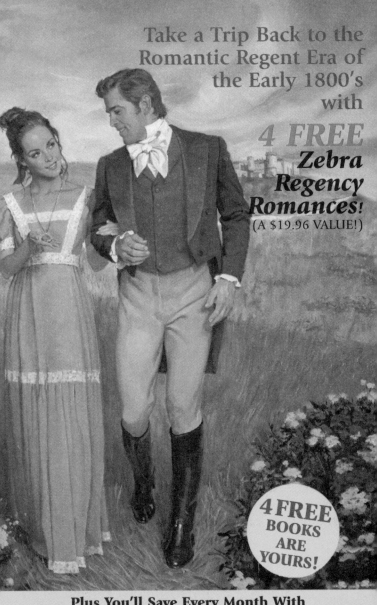

Take a Trip Back to the
Romantic Regent Era of
the Early 1800's
with

4 FREE
Zebra
Regency
Romances!
(A $19.96 VALUE!)

4 FREE BOOKS ARE YOURS!

**Plus You'll Save Every Month With
Convenient Home Delivery!**

We'd Like to Invite You to Subscribe to Zebra's Regency Romance Book Club and Send You 4 Free Books as Your Introduction! (Worth $19.96!)

If you're a Regency lover, imagine the joy of getting 4 FREE Zebra Regency Romances and then the chance to have these lovely stories delivered to your home each month at the lowest price available! Well, that's our offer to you and here's how you benefit by becoming a Regency Romance subscriber:

- *4 FREE Introductory Regency Romances are delivered to your doorstep (you only pay for shipping & handling)*

- *4 BRAND NEW Regencies are then delivered each month (usually before they're available in bookstores)*

- *Subscribers save almost $4.00 off the cover price every month*

- *You also receive a FREE monthly newsletter, which features author profiles, discounts, subscriber benefits, book previews and more*

- *There's no risks or obligations…in other words, you can cancel whenever you wish with no questions asked*

Join the thousands of readers who enjoy the savings and convenience offered to Regency Romance subscribers. After your initial introductory shipment, you'll receive 4 brand-new Zebra Regency Romances each month to examine for 10 days. Then, if you decide to keep the books, you pay the preferred subscriber's price, plus shipping and handling.

It's a no-lose proposition, so return the FREE BOOK CERTIFICATE today!

4 **FREE BOOKS** are waiting for you! Just mail in the certificate below!

FREE BOOK CERTIFICATE

YES! Please rush me 4 FREE Zebra Regency Romances (I only pay $1.99 for shipping and handling).I understand that each month thereafter I will be able to preview 4 brand-new Regency Romances FREE for 10 days. Then, if I should decide to keep them, I will pay the money-saving preferred subscriber's price for all 4… (that's a savings of 20% off the retail price), plus shipping and handling. I may return any shipment within 10 days and owe nothing, and I may cancel this subscription at any time.

Name _____

Address _____ Apt. _____

City _____ State _____ Zip _____

Telephone (___) _____

Signature _____
(If under 18, parent or guardian must sign)

Offer limited to one per household and not to current subscribers. Terms,
offer and prices subject to change. Orders subject to acceptance by
Regency Romance Book Club. Offer Valid in the U.S. only.   RN053A

Treat yourself to 4 FREE Regency Romances!
A $19.96 VALUE... FREE!
No obligation to buy anything ever!

ally his parents, and less frequently his tutor. Now, however, he saw the whole world differently.

"Nonsense, Theodore, you are just a little boy! You have no notion of what is amusing!" replied his affectionate mother.

"You are out there, ma'am," said Belvedere abruptly. "The boy is right. It is damned amusing!"

Lucy looked horrified, whether because of his lapse in language or because of his failure to agree with her was unclear. "Really, Mr. Belvedere! You are a guest in this house—" she began, but she was interrupted.

Nigel had stood at his place and was tapping his spoon on the edge of his wine glass, and the ringing stilled the conversations.

"I believe that we should put it to a vote," he announced. "We will go round the table and determine who was amused." He turned to bow to his mother. "Mama, if you will please begin."

"With pleasure, Nigel," she said, smiling at her youngest. "I was most certainly amused."

Charles stood, glancing across the table at his wife. "I fear Lucy has little humor. I must apologize for her. I agree with Mama."

Sally lifted her glass in a toast to her younger brothers. "Thoroughly amusing," she said, smiling.

Nigel was next, and he stood and bowed. "I feel that Monty and I should not vote—although we, of course, were thoroughly amused." He was seated to a brief burst of applause.

Olivia stood. "Wonderful!" she exclaimed. "Of course it was delightful. Nigel and Monty could not be other than amusing."

"Monty is not voting and we will skip the lower part of the table for the moment," he said, bowing to the younger portion of the family. "Edward, you are next."

"Amusing," he returned. "How could it be otherwise?"

Lucy, seated next to him, frowned. "You know very well what I think," she replied.

To the pleasure of everyone—except Lucy—Walter Belvedere repeated his opinion, raising his glass in a toast as he did so. "Damned amusing!" he repeated.

Elise stood next. "This is one of the reasons I always long to come to London," she said. "Monty and Nigel, you are a constant delight."

"And now," said Nigel, "let us hear from the lower end of the table. Let me hear from those of you that did not think Monty and I were amusing."

There was a moment of complete silence. Then Nigel said, "And now, let me hear from those of you that enjoyed what Monty and I had to say." There followed a minute of clapping, whooping, foot-stamping, and barking.

Nigel bowed to Lucy, then to Ravinia before seating himself. "I rest my case," he concluded.

Ravinia smiled and lifted her glass to her two younger sons, a gesture that everyone at the table—except Lucy—duplicated immediately.

Elise touched the rim of her glass to that of Mr. Belvedere's. For the moment he seemed almost like an approachable person. She knew that was not really the case, but for the moment, it was true.

"And, Miss MacGregor," said Mr. Belvedere, after they had drunk the toast, "I suppose that the other reasons you enjoy coming to London are to go to the shops so that you can buy pretty trinkets and furbelows to adorn yourself and to enjoy the fulsome attentions of rattle-pated young men who spend their time dealing in false coin."

"Rattle-pated!" she replied sharply, in a voice that she hoped was low enough to avoid being heard by the others. "You have once again overstepped yourself, Mr. Belvedere. You have no idea what you are talking about!"

Walter Belvedere merely shrugged, and Elise was prevented from saying anything more by her aunt's announcement that the ladies would now retire to the drawing room. Elise seethed silently as she left the drawing room, refusing even to glance at Mr. Belvedere. Not, she knew very well, that her action would perturb him at all. Doubtless he would not even notice it.

Ravinia, on the other hand, was very pleased with the events at dinner. She had never seen Walter Belvedere so engaged with other people. Things were going exceedingly well.

Eleven

Elise expected the rest of the evening to be unbearable, but, to her surprise, her anger cooled as events unfolded. Marjorie once again retired to the pianoforte to serenade them, and her gentle playing served to soothe some of her hot resentment of Mr. Belvedere's unjustified remarks about James Gray. She knew, of course, that Mr. Gray was a very intelligent man, even if Walter Belvedere did not, and she had no reason to believe that Mr. Gray was a common flirt, as Belvedere's comment had indicated. The misunderstanding, she decided, stemmed from Mr. Belvedere's lack of knowledge of the gentleman in question and from his own pitiable lack of social skills. By the time Marjorie began playing "Green Groweth the Holly," Elise's mood had softened considerably.

Nigel, entering the drawing room just then with the rest of the gentlemen, exclaimed, "Come now, Marjorie, you must begin again so that Elise can sing for us."

Elise started to refuse, but Monty, recognizing her expression, grinned at her and said, "Do sing for us, cousin. Help the evening along."

When she still looked doubtful, he urged her again, "Still the season, after all. Haven't had Twelfth Night yet."

Finally giving way, she smiled at him and at Marjorie, who was watching her anxiously. Marjorie enjoyed performing for company, and she had developed a great admiration for Elise and Olivia. Elise knew that she would be making at least two people happy by singing.

As she stood to take her place beside the pianoforte, Nigel said, "Naturally, we cannot hope to equal Mr. Gray's performance *after* you sing the song this time, but just like that gentleman, many of us find this a favorite holiday piece. Merely pretend that he is here, cousin. You may sing tenderly to me as though I were Mr. Gray."

His comment elicited choked laughter from Reginald and Theodore, which was cut off by a swift signal from their grandmother. Elise's cheeks were flaming by the time Marjorie had played the opening chords, and it was with some difficulty that she began. For a moment she closed her eyes, imagining only the intent gaze of James Gray as he had watched her the last time she had sung. That helped to steady her, and as she moved into the second stanza, she looked only at the younger children or Monty or Ravinia, for she knew that none of them would overset her.

When the last note had died away, Nigel cried, "Bravo, my cousin and my niece! Now if only Mr. Gray were here, the kissing bough could be put to its proper use!"

Reginald and Theodore once again gave way to snickering, the sort that belongs to young boys who are just now aware that kissing a girl is something that lies in their near future. Elise flushed again and tried to ignore his comment and their laughter.

Monty, attempting to be of service, said, "Kissed her because he has good taste, Nigel. Would have done it myself if I'd thought of it."

Here Elise discomposed him entirely by walking directly to him and kissing him on the cheek, then seating herself by Charles. Reginald and Theodore, joined by Lionel, Nelson, and Niles, who took their lead from the older boys, gave way completely at this provocation and could not be called to order for several minutes, so music was abandoned and a more energetic outlet for their spirits was sought.

"Whatever are we going to do with them?" said Sally, gazing with dismay at the children, all of whom had now succumbed to hilarity and showed no signs of recovery. Even the sedate Marjorie, mimicked by Tillie, laughed until the tears ran down her cheeks. Bangs naturally took exception to such a display and barked unceasingly—brief, staccato, imperative commands to desist. The children paid no attention to them.

"I could have told you that this would happen if you did not show more restraint in your behavior!" said Lucy virtuously.

"And what do you mean by that?" demanded Sally. "That Elise should not have sung? That she should not have kissed Monty? That we should all sit here with our hands folded neatly in our laps and never move until you have given us leave to do so?" She turned on her sister-in-law in a fury. "If you could keep your children under control, the little ones would not be behaving like this!"

Lucy turned an unattractive beet red. "They are just high-spirited boys!" she retorted. "If Nigel and Monty showed at least a degree of restraint in their behavior, this scene would not be taking place!"

Here she walked over to Reginald to attempt to make him stop laughing. Reginald, however, seemed far beyond help, and Theodore ignored her altogether.

"You see?" she cried sharply, her face flushed with anger. "They will not listen to me, and who is to blame for that?"

The others stared at her, and she turned, in a frenzy of anger, to Monty and Nigel. "They are the ones!" she exclaimed bitterly. "They are the ones that teach the boys to disregard what they have been taught and to behave in such a vulgar manner!"

Monty and Nigel stared at her, startled, and Ravinia said, "Come now, Lucy, you must not be hysterical when you are disappointed in the behavior of your children."

Here Lucy unwisely turned upon her mother-in-law. "If you provided a climate proper for young boys to prosper, they would not be misbehaving in such a manner! They do so because their uncles set them a poor example and you uphold them!"

At this point, she flung herself from the room—which was wise, for Ravinia might well have provided her with a means of exit. When she left, a sudden silence descended upon the drawing room, for even the boys regained control of themselves after Lucy's emotional exit.

"Got just the ticket!" said Monty.

Everyone stared at him, but he was unperturbed.

"Jackstraws!" he said briskly. "Just the thing!"

Elise stared at him in admiration. It was, she thought as she watched them all busily engrossed in the game just a few minutes later, indeed just the thing required to calm their tumultuous spirits.

Marjorie had raced to the schoolroom to gather up the box containing the hook and the slender sticks used to play the game. When she returned, Monty had gathered all the children in a circle, as well as Olivia and Sally, who wished to play also, and Nigel, who did not wish to play but was forced to do so by the others. Elise and Ravinia sat watching them while Charles and Edward retired to the safety of the fireside to read. Mr. Belvedere had risen and started for the library, but Ravinia had called him to her side, reminding him that she might well discover other ancient delights among the boxes she was sorting through and "inviting" him to be seated and watch the progress of the game. He looked pained, a fact which did not escape Elise's notice and was a source of secret delight, but he did as his hostess requested.

As the children watched intently, Monty held the clutch of thin, colored sticks a foot above the carpet and suddenly released them, so that they formed a hopeless tangle. Then he announced that he would go first, and the rest would take their turns in alphabetical order, an announcement that caused the others to protest loudly and demand to know why he should go first.

He raised his hand for silence, and the children stopped to listen to him. Elise wished that Lucy were present to see how readily they gave him their attention now that he had won them over; it might offer her a clearer view of her unfair assessment of the situation than any amount of talking would.

"My idea," he pointed out to them briefly.

After a moment of thought, Reginald and Theodore looked at each other and shrugged. "It's fair," agreed Theodore, and he and the others settled down for serious play.

Elise watched in amusement as Monty bent close to the stack and eyed the position of the various sticks carefully, trying to decide which one could be removed most easily. The object, of course, was to remove as many sticks as possible without moving any of the others save the one, and to be the player with the greatest number of sticks when the last one was picked up. Players did not have to relinquish their turn until they accidentally moved a stick other than the one they were attempting to remove.

It was clear to the onlookers that Monty had no intention of giving away the game to the children. He first picked up the one stick that had flung itself free of the others and put it in front of him.

Reginald snorted. "Taking candy from a baby!"

Monty eyed him. "Wish me to leave it there like a cawker?" he demanded. "Would you?"

Reginald shook his head, and Monty settled in to

choose his next stick. He lay with the side of his face directly on the carpet, sizing up the situation carefully, and the children, even Tillie, all attempted to do the same thing. After a minute of careful thought, Monty slid the hook cautiously around a scarlet stick propped against two others at the edge of the stack. It did not appear to be supporting any other stick, and he very slowly moved it away from the others. When he had it safely away, all of the players exhaled as one, for they had all been holding their breath.

Elise knew that, had Monty treated the game carelessly, the children would have done so as well. By taking his play so seriously, it was clear to them that they were pitted against one another in a real game of skill. The boys immediately assumed the same attitude they had toward billiards.

Monty caused movement with his third stick, and so the hook passed to Marjorie, who astonished the others by her dexterity, expertly fishing out four sticks before losing her turn. The younger boys and Tillie had not yet developed the physical control necessary to play the game really well and their mother was a passable player, but the older boys, Nigel, and Olivia were quick and deft.

At the end of the game, Marjorie emerged the winner, to the great distress of her brothers, who demanded a second round. Nigel managed to extricate himself at that point, but Monty, Sally, and Olivia had become intensely involved in the game. Play continued for quite some time, periods of attentive silence punctuated with cries of victory or despair. When Reginald hooked the pickpole around a stick at the base of the stack and brought down all the others, there was a cry of outrage.

"Clodpole!" exclaimed Theodore, staring at his brother in disbelief. "How could you make so corkbrained a move?"

Monty turned to Theodore and stared at him for a moment without saying a word.

Theodore flushed and gave his attention to his fingernails. "Sorry, Reg," he murmured. "I didn't mean it."

Monty nodded in satisfaction at his apology. "Heat of the game," he said. "Still, must remember you are a gentleman."

The others nodded, and the game continued apace until Ravinia announced that it was time for the children to go to bed. There was heavy protest, but they at last gave it up when Ravinia promised them that there would be games again the next afternoon and evening. Sally and the older children accepted their candles from the footman waiting at the base of the stairs, and lighted their way up to bed.

Mr. Belvedere turned to Ravinia and bowed briefly, saying, "I trust that since the children have been excused to go to bed, I may also be excused to go to the library."

Ravinia smiled and took the distinct liberty of patting his arm. "Beavers is just coming in to lay a late supper for us, Mr. Belvedere. Do stay for that."

Here she rose and went to one of the windows, pulling aside the curtain. "And I understand that the snow shows not the slightest sign of letting up just yet," she added. "Beavers said that when one of the kitchen maids opened the rear door to try to reach the dustbin, there was a bank of snow against the door that came above her waist. Between the great amount of snow and the wind blowing it into drifts, you will unquestionably be with us tomorrow, too. I do think that you should have your supper and then go to your chamber to sleep tonight."

Ravinia sounded distinctly like a mother, Elise thought, and Mr. Belvedere was not only too old to listen to his mother about such things but also too difficult to allow his own mother or anyone else to make such a suggestion to him. She waited with interest to see how he would respond.

Before he could say anything, however, Monty intervened. "Should get some sleep," he counseled seriously. "Might bring on a fit of the ague."

Everyone looked mildly startled by his contribution, but he had clearly been giving the matter some thought.

"Don't worry about your gear. Borrow from one of my brothers." He paused and studied Charles a moment. "About his size. Have Beavers bring you what you need."

"That is very kind of you, Longfellow," replied Mr. Belvedere, looking surprised. The rest of them looked even more surprised, not only because Monty had devoted some thought to the matter but also because Belvedere had been courteous.

Pleased with himself, Monty addressed himself happily to a substantial supper of deviled kidneys and stewed cheese while the others served their plates and enjoyed their final repast for the evening.

Elise, not at all hungry, had moved to one of the windows, pulling back the curtain and trying to catch a glimpse of the snow through the frosted panes.

"I had thought of attempting to walk home tomorrow," said Belvedere, surprising her by joining her there. "However, it does not appear that will be possible."

"Not unless you wish to lose your way and freeze to death in one of the drifts," she responded crisply, sounding as though she quite relished the thought.

There was a brief pause. "That has never been one of my desires," he replied, a slight note of amusement in his tone. "I am pleased to hear you express concern for my well-being, however."

"You mistook my meaning," she reassured him. "I was merely making an observation."

"Fair enough," he said. After a brief pause, during which they both attempted to stare through the frosted panes, he said idly, "I understand you are to be married in March, Miss MacGregor. My felicitations."

Taken by surprise, Elise merely nodded.

They remained at the window in silence for a few minutes more.

Finally, he cleared his throat slightly and murmured, "I believe that I will take your aunt's advice and retire to the chamber that has been prepared for me, but before I leave, Miss MacGregor, I would like to leave you with a question that has occurred to me, and which might be of some interest to you."

"Indeed, Mr. Belvedere?" she replied, more surprised than ever.

"Does Mr. Gray, who pays you such fulsome compliments, know that you are about to be married?"

Elise stared at him in consternation, but Mr. Belvedere merely bowed and silently left the room.

Elise remained at the window for some time, staring blankly ahead. As she thought through the events of the past few days, she reached a most unsettling conclusion.

She had not the slightest idea what the answer to his question was.

Twelve

Elise slept very little that night. First she thought about her father and Mr. Westbrook receiving their letters. If they had not been slowed by the storm, the letters would both by now have reached their destinations. Elise clutched the covers under her chin as she pictured her father reading her words after his exhausting journey home.

How could she have been so thoughtless in her timing? What if he fell ill after this final blow? She should have considered matters more carefully before she had written those letters. She was forever preaching to her sister to use self-restraint and to avoid theatrical gestures. What had she herself done? Tossing convulsively, she finally rose from the bed despite the cold so that she would not awaken Olivia and have to explain her restlessness.

Her mind turned to Mr. Westbrook and his letter. She added some coals to the fire and pulled her chair close to it, wrapping herself in her dressing gown and a lap robe. Mr. Westbrook would not take the news well, she knew. It would be a blow to his pride. She shivered a moment, thinking of it. She was grateful that she was not at home so that he could come directly to Brookston Hall and confront her.

Then a thought occurred to her that she had not considered before: Mr. Westbrook would go directly to her father to express his displeasure. He, instead of the guilty Elise, would be the one to bear the brunt of Westbrook's anger and indignation.

Horrified by her thoughtlessness, Elise wept bitterly, but finally forced herself to stop. There could be no advantage in this, she told herself. It could not help her father. What was done, was done. All that she could do now was to concentrate on the future.

Despite her misgivings and her misery at the thought of the distress she was causing her father, she was still determined that she would not marry Mr. Westbrook. She had decided that firmly and she knew that her decision was correct, no matter how discomfiting its results. She had been foolish to accept, but she had finally done the proper thing in notifying him of her refusal.

Then she considered Mr. Belvedere's question, which she had forced to the back of her thoughts. Did Mr. Gray indeed know that she was engaged? And, if he did, what precisely did his actions mean?

She was afraid to think this question through to any logical conclusion. Exhausted, she crawled back into bed beside Olivia, savoring the warmth and gratefully giving way to sleep. She could consider her problem no longer. She would think about it tomorrow, when her mind was fresh.

When the sisters arose the next morning, they could still hear the wind and the blowing snow.

"Do you think it will ever end?" whispered Olivia, as they lay within their curtained bed in comparative warmth. "Beavers says that none of them can ever remember such a storm as this in London."

"Of course it will end," replied Elise briskly, forcing herself to sit up and greet the morning. "In another week, I daresay we shall laugh at ourselves for being worried, and will tell stories about what we did while the storm continued."

And continue it most certainly did. When Monty attempted to open the front door that morning, the experience of the kitchen maid the night before was duplicated, only Monty was facing a shoulder-high drift of snow. As he attempted to peer through the driving flakes, he reported to Nigel, who was substantially shorter, and to Beavers, who was hovering nearby, that there was no sign of life. Indeed, Monty told them, he could not tell where the street left off and the garden in the middle of the square began. Everything had become a whirling whiteness.

"And so, dear companions," said Nigel at breakfast, recounting the events of the early morning, "we find ourselves adrift in a sea of white."

The others, with the exception of Monty, stared at him.

"Nigel, precisely what does that mean?" demanded his sister Sally. "Are we to live the rest of our lives here in Darlington Square with Mama? Or shall we run short of supplies and all die, so that only our bones are found when the spring thaw occurs?"

"Sally, I had forgotten what a constant delight you are," responded Nigel. "I assure you that we shall not perish here. If I must sacrifice Charles's firstborn child so that we may all make our escape, I shall do so. The gods must be satisfied!"

Charles looked mildly interested at this. "I shouldn't think that Reggie would give way to being sacrificed too easily, Nigel," he commented comfortably. "Just a word of caution, you understand."

Elise and Olivia chuckled at this interchange, but not everyone at the table was amused.

"Really!" exclaimed Lucy indignantly, her lips thinning until it scarcely appeared she had any. "Charles, how can you speak of the death of your own child so lightly? And why do the rest of you encourage the two of them by laughing? What is the matter with this family that you seem to have not the least notion of what is proper and fitting behavior?"

Nigel looked at Lucy with interest. "I do assure you, Lucy, that I would not sacrifice Reginald without giving due consideration to the matter." Turning to his brother, he added, " And I do appreciate, Charles, your word of caution about Reggie's disinclination to be sacrificed. I will take all of that into account, I do assure you."

"Charles!" said Lucy sharply. "Why will you do nothing to stop such monstrous comments about your own child? What sort of unnatural parent are you?"

Charles appeared to give the matter serious thought. "I am not an unnatural parent, Lucy," he said clearly. "I am a most reasonable man. If my brother makes it clear to me that Reggie must be sacrificed so that we may all survive this ordeal, then who am I to quibble? There are others to be thought of as well. We must not be selfish."

Charles settled back into his chair, his eyes twinkling, but Lucy, literal to the core, was horrified.

"So you would speak of sacrificing your child for the well-being of yourself and others?" she demanded. "What if I were to tell you, Charles, that I will make known your outrageous behavior from one end of town to the other? Perhaps that would stop you!"

Charles shrugged. "I would advise you not to waste your energy, Lucy dear," he said, sinking back into his chair to read the paper from two days earlier for the twelfth time. "I believe that my outrageous behavior has been the subject of conversation for some years. Gossips prefer fresh *on-dits.* "

Walter Belvedere strolled in the room at this unfortunate juncture, knowing nothing of what had transpired, and was set upon by Lucy.

"Mr. Belvedere!" she fairly shrieked, casting herself upon him. "You are the only outsider here in the midst of this monstrous family! You must help me protect my young!"

Belvedere looked about him for the source of the threat as he gently loosed Lucy's grip upon his sleeve. "From what must they be protected, ma'am?" He looked about the room again and turned to Lucy. "Where *are* your young, madam?" he inquired.

Lucy clutched his arm again. "Upstairs sleeping, I should imagine," she replied in a shrill voice.

Belvedere stared at her for a moment. "Then I take it they are safe, ma'am?" he inquired. "I see no sign of bandits, dragons, or rabid dogs," he added, again gently detaching her hand from his sleeve.

"You haven't checked Bangs," pointed out Nigel in a reasonable tone. "For all we know, he is upstairs foaming at the mouth as he waits for Tillie to feed him her breakfast."

"You see!" Lucy said bitterly, directing her comment to Walter Belvedere. "How can he say such a thing about a defenseless child?"

"Lucy, you know that Tillie is perfectly safe, that Bangs is not rabid, and that Nigel is only joking," said Elise. "There is no reason to be so distressed."

"No reason to be distressed!" Lucy exclaimed in disbelief. "How can I not be distressed when the very lives of children are talked about so lightly?"

"But, Mrs. Longfellow," began Belvedere, "as Miss MacGregor pointed out, I am certain that the comment was made only in jest."

"But don't you see what an unsuitable jest it was, sir?" Lucy demanded of him, fairly wringing the sleeve of his jacket in her anger. "And you have not heard the worst of their horrible jokes."

"Well-made jacket!" exclaimed Monty suddenly, troubled by her attack upon Belvedere's sleeve. "Looks every which way now, though! Best let go of it, Lucy!" He was clearly acutely distressed by Lucy's desecration of Belvedere's well-cut jacket.

Lucy naturally paid no attention to Monty. Her focus was entirely upon Mr. Belvedere.

"And what is the worst of it, ma'am?" he asked patiently, reseating her at her place and serving his plate as he attempted to make sense of her words. The others, including Ravinia and Theodore, just arrived in the doorway, were watching the scene with interest.

"Nigel is amusing himself by saying he must sacrifice Reginald in order to put an end to the snow!" she shrilled. "He said that the gods must be satisfied!"

Belvedere looked startled, but he seated himself at the table and glanced inquiringly at Nigel.

"And so they must," agreed Nigel, calmly buttering a muffin. "After all, we can't have this snow go on forever, Belvedere. I refuse to live the rest of my life walled in by snow and surrounded by children. Something must be done. I understand it's best in such cases to sacrifice the firstborn child. I'm certain that you see that."

"You do have a point," Belvedere said, nodding and smiling faintly now that he understood what was going on.

Lucy gasped in indignant disbelief at his response, but the others were clearly amused.

"Warned him that Reggie won't go peacefully," said Charles from behind his paper.

"Bad storm," observed Monty thoughtfully, entering into the spirit of things. "Might need more than one. Best take Theo, too!" Here he grinned at his nephew, whom he had seen peeking around Ravinia.

"How can you say such things?" Lucy demanded angrily and rose from her chair again, this time turning to march from the room as the others gave way to laughter.

Ravinia, just entering with Theodore in her wake,

stopped her daughter-in-law. "Lucy, you must compose yourself," she said in a low voice. "Come back in and be seated."

"Just what has been happening in here?" she then demanded of the others, quite as though she didn't know.

Sally shrugged. "Nigel merely observed that we might have to sacrifice Charles's firstborn in order to stop the snow," she explained briefly. "Lucy went all to pieces."

"I warned him that Reggie could be a problem, Mama," said Charles virtuously from behind his paper. "Can't say I didn't warn 'im."

Nigel glanced at Theodore, who had been listening with interest, but who took advantage of the break in conversation to bring up his own concerns.

"Uncle Monty, may we play billiards this morning?" he demanded.

Monty nodded, and Nigel eyed Theodore thoughtfully. "Perhaps you would like to be the sacrifice to stop the snow, Theo?" Nigel inquired. "No need for us to go to all the trouble of going upstairs to fetch Reggie."

Theodore shook his head and grinned, clearly untroubled by the remark.

"No time. Reg and I are going to play billiards with Uncle Monty. Perhaps after billiards," he replied, turning to gallop back upstairs with the good news.

"Well, there it is," sighed Nigel. "We have no sacrifice. The snow will never end. We shall all dwindle away into old age here together." He shuddered briefly. "I believe I shall have more coffee."

"I do not understand why you must make a mockery—" began Lucy angrily, rising once more from her chair.

Before Lucy could say anything else, Ravinia took her arm and guided her gently to the doorway. "Do go upstairs and rest now, Lucy. I shall have some tea sent up to you." Lucy knew that her mother-in-law was ordering her to leave, not asking her to do so. She did not truly wish to stay, but she did wish to have the last word, so she departed very reluctantly, casting an angry glance at the others.

A brief silence fell over the group as Ravinia served her plate and joined them at the table. To everyone's surprise, it was Mr. Belvedere who broke it.

"I know that I am considered an oddity," he observed thoughtfully, appearing to address no one in particular. "After seeing all of you today, I cannot tell you what a comfort it is to know that I am not alone."

A brief silence followed his statement as the others recovered from their shock, and then an explosion of laughter rocked the room, bringing Beavers to the door at the double-quick. To his amazement, everyone at the table—except for Mr. Belvedere, who was calmly eating his breakfast—had dissolved in laughter. Even his mistress, normally the picture of self-control, was wiping her eyes with a handkerchief.

"Very good, Belvedere!" Nigel finally managed to gasp. "I'd no idea you had it in you!"

"Collection of oddities," chortled Monty. "Shall never be able to look round the table again without thinking of it."

Thus, everyone—except Lucy, of course—began the day in spirits. After breakfast, Monty, the children, and the much-maligned Bangs retired to the billiards room once more, Monty intent upon honing some of the skills he had taught his protégée yesterday. Mr. Belvedere naturally retired happily to the library once more, and Ravinia had a fire lighted in the morning room so that she could go over her household accounts and discuss the state of the household larder with the cook. Lucy had remained in her chamber, and the others adjourned to the drawing room to read or play cards, and so whiled away the rest of the day quite peacefully.

When they were all, including the children, gathered

once more in the drawing room after dinner, however, a certain restlessness fell upon them. Jackstraws was not an option for the evening, for after billiards, Monty and the children had played game after game until Reginald and Theodore had each been able to defeat their younger sister at least once.

Marjorie proudly wore a small crown, made of gold paper from the schoolroom, which Monty had insisted upon making for her to indicate that she was the Queen of Jackstraws. Fortunately, Theodore felt that he was too old for such things, for if he had demanded a similar crown for his prowess with a cue, trouble would certainly have come upon them. Reginald had not yet discovered an area, other than age, in which he could establish himself as the superior of the other two. Since he had long been accustomed to asserting his authority over them, he was growing defensive as Theo and Marjorie both found areas in which they excelled. Already Monty had been obliged to remind Reggie that a cue was not the same thing as a sword, for he had attempted to challenge Theo to a duel in the billiards room.

Ravinia, taking note of the restlessness, announced, "I thought that this evening we would all play charades—and to close it, the children have been requesting a game of blindman's buff."

This news was well received, although Charles and Nigel looked longingly at the whist table and Mr. Belvedere at the door leading to the library. Ravinia, however, established eye contact with all of them, and soon the entire group had settled down to serious play.

To their amazement, Monty and Elise emerged as the shining lights of the evening. Monty pantomimed to perfection Lady MacBeth's dagger scene as the key to the play's title. As he sat down to general laughter and applause, he preened himself a little, grinning.

"I know that you never read the play, Monty, and I cannot imagine that you ever went to see it, so how in thunder did you know to do that scene?" demanded Nigel, keenly aware of his brother's lack of literary expertise.

"Accident. Forced to see Mrs. Siddons perform it once," Monty explained. "Wanted to arrive just in time for the farce, but got there too early. Trapped."

"Well, it obviously made a deep impression upon you," said Olivia, "for you were splendid in the part."

"Private," replied Monty, looking anxious. "No need for anyone outside the family to know."

"Mr. Belvedere knows," pointed out Olivia, glancing at that gentlemen.

"Ah yes, but that is no problem," Elise assured him. "You will recall, Monty, that we count Mr. Belvedere as one of ourselves."

There was a brief pause and Monty looked momentarily puzzled. Then understanding dawned and he grinned. "Oddity!" he exclaimed. "Just so!"

"You understand, Belvedere, that being included in such a group as this is a dubious honor," said Nigel.

Belvedere nodded. "I am fully aware of that," he assured Nigel. "In fact, it has occurred to me that the association might be harmful to my reputation."

Laughter greeted his response, but Lucy said in an annoyed tone, "I cannot see what is laughable about an insult to the reputation of this family."

At this, the laughter increased and Elise, taking pity upon Lucy, patted her on the arm and whispered, "Try not to make such a fuss, Lucy. Pray do not dwell upon the matter. You simply make yourself unhappy."

Fortunately, Lucy allowed the matter to rest, and Elise stood up to take her turn at charades. In record time, she performed Caesar's famous quotation, "I came, I saw, I conquered." Pointing to her eye for the first, third, and fifth words was truly enough of an indication, but she very quickly rolled Theo, who was seated on the floor, onto his stomach and placed her foot upon his back, her arms raised above her in victory.

Flushed with the ease of her success—and the effort of rolling Theo over—she returned to her seat, her eyes bright and her cheeks pink. Hers was the final pantomime, and Ravinia announced that there was time for a brief game of blindman's buff before the children retired.

There was an immediate scrambling as people rose and the ladies hurried to move any breakables to a place of safety. Once all looked secure, Ravinia turned to the group.

"And who shall be the blindman first?" she asked, holding up the white kerchief she had brought down with her. "We shall have three, I think, before bedtime."

There was a great outcry among the young, but Lionel was chosen first. Ravinia bound the cloth snugly around his eyes, turned him around three times, and gave him a gentle push into the room. The others scrambled, but Lionel was very quick on his feet—too quick, in fact, for he bumped into a piecrust table and tripped across a footstool. Fortunately, he did himself no severe damage, and he was up and moving quickly again in a cat's whisker. The joy of the chase was great, and the others laughed and called to him and occasionally ran just behind him. Finally he managed to whirl quickly enough on one such occasion, and caught Reginald. Then Lionel reached up and patted Reggie's face, running his fingers lightly across it, then felt his way down his brother's jacket sleeve until he encountered a bandage on his right hand.

"It's Reginald!" he shouted. "Thought it might have been Theo, but then I remembered you'd burned yourself yesterday!"

"Probably trying to throw a hot coal at someone," murmured Monty to Nigel. His relationship with the children had greatly improved, but Reginald was still occasionally a thorn.

Once Reginald was securely blindfolded, the chase began once more, this time with increased vigor, for Reginald was a larger and a faster blindman. In the midst of the screaming and running and protests that peeking wasn't fair, Monty dashed directly past his elbow, daring Reggie to catch him, and Reggie turned quickly and lunged in that direction. He missed Monty, but he captured Mr. Belvedere, who had withdrawn to the side of the room and had merely been watching the game.

"Got you!" exclaimed Reginald, pouncing.

Mr. Belvedere stood perfectly still and silent as Reginald invaded his privacy by patting his shoulder.

"A gentleman," said Reginald astutely, "but too tall for Nigel and heavier shoulders than anyone except my father or Mr. Belvedere."

There was a pause while the boy knelt down and patted the gentleman's boots. "It's Mr. Belvedere!" he announced triumphantly. "My father is wearing Hessians, and Mr. Belvedere has on high-tops!"

"I would be happy to relinquish my turn to someone else," said Belvedere, glancing around the group.

"Nonsense, Mr. Belvedere!" exclaimed Ravinia. "This will be good for you. Here, bend your head a bit, please, so that I may blindfold you."

Perhaps because of the angle at which she was tying the blindfold or perhaps because it slipped, the others were soon certain that their blindman was not truly blinded by the kerchief. Three times he almost caught someone, then turned away at the last possible moment with no good reason for changing course. Finally he caught Elise in the circle of his arms.

"It is a lady," he said with certainty, in the midst of laughter.

Here he gently patted her curls. "And she is wearing her hair up, but then so are all the other ladies."

He cupped his hand round the side of her face, his fingers lightly touching her cheek. "And she is short and her face is small, so I know that this must be either Miss MacGregor or Miss Olivia, for all the other ladies are taller."

"I am stunned by your powers of observation, Belvedere," called Nigel. "I was not certain that you even knew our names. You continue to amaze us."

Belvedere ignored him as he caught up Elise's hands and ran his fingers over them. "She is wearing a ring with a square-cut stone on her right hand, little finger," he announced. "It is Miss MacGregor."

A round of applause succeeded his identification of her, although Reginald was calling out, "It's a hoax! You could see through the blindfold!" Ravinia called him to order and instructed Beavers to bring in their late supper and to have the children's refreshments sent up to the nursery.

Mr. Belvedere seated himself next to Elise, who was recovering from the excitement of the chase, her eyes still bright and her cheeks glowing.

He looked at her for a moment, then said, "You need no pearls, Miss MacGregor."

Elise stared at him. "What do you mean, Mr. Belvedere?" she asked. "No one was speaking of pearls."

"I was," he replied. "You need no pearls to emphasize the glow of your skin and your hair, as Mr. Gray told you."

Realizing suddenly what he was speaking of, she colored.

"You see?" he said quietly. "Mr. Gray was incorrect. The pearls would not emphasize that glow. Your skin and hair and eyes would cause the pearls to look dull against their luster."

He stood quickly, bowing to her and to her hostess,

then excused himself to Ravinia, saying that he was not feeling well and would go early to bed that night.

Elise sat perfectly still, shocked by such a comment from such a man. Nigel came over and took Belvedere's place, looking after him.

"Quite a surprising fellow, isn't he?" he remarked.

Elise nodded. "Oh yes, he most certainly is, Nigel. Words fail me."

She was still mulling over his unexpected compliment when she went to sleep that evening. She had examined it suspiciously from every angle possible, certain that it must be an insult disguised as a pleasantry, but she could not see that it was anything other than an extraordinary compliment from a man who paid none.

Thirteen

Morning finally brought relief from the storm. When Elise awoke, the first thing that she became aware of was the silence. Darlington Square was normally a quiet enough spot, but recently the sound of the wind and snow had been so constant a part of the background that she had ceased to notice it. This morning there was no sound.

"Livy!" she said, poking her sister, who was still snuggled beneath the covers. "Listen!"

"Listen to what?" she responded sleepily, opening only one eye to peer at Elise. "I don't hear anything."

"That's what I mean, Livy. The storm must be over."

The two of them went to the frost-covered window, trying to peer out, but they could see nothing. Elise tried to raise the window, which seemed to be frozen in place. After a brief struggle with both girls working, they managed to raise it a few inches, and a small avalanche of snow fell onto the carpet.

They jumped back, but then Elise put out her hand and swept the sill free of snow, this time knocking it outside the window. Shivering, she knelt and gathered up most of the snow that had fallen to the carpet and flung it outside, too. Then, still kneeling so that she could see out the few inches of opening they had cleared, she peered out.

"Nigel was right, Livy," she said. "We are surrounded

by a sea of white. Why, I can't even tell clearly where the trees are in the park. The wind has swept the snow into such odd drifts that it is difficult to tell what is beneath the snow."

"Let me see!" Livy demanded, braving the cold to kneel beside her sister and stare out across the square. "Not a person to be seen," she murmured.

"Nor a carriage or cart," agreed Elise. "But now that the snow has stopped, I daresay it won't be long until the sweepers are out. Businessmen will be anxious to get back to their offices, and doctors will need to visit the sick."

"And the cooks will need to send to the butchers and the greengrocers," added Olivia. "And perhaps we will be able to get out for a bit today, too—although it is still shockingly cold."

When they arrived downstairs, they discovered that Beavers had sent two young footmen out the front door and two out the back door, with orders to clear a path. Obediently, the young men had plunged out into the cold and were busily burrowing through the banks of snow.

The two in front had made enough progress so that a person might just step out the door and look around. Monty, who had just been out in Nigel's greatcoat, came in hurriedly, closing the door behind him and clapping his hands against his arms.

"Devilish cold!" he announced unnecessarily, seeing his cousins. "Should see the icicles! Looked up and very nearly fell into a fit!"

"Fell into a fit over icicles?" responded Olivia. "Why, Monty?"

"Long!" he answered. "Some of them very nearly as tall as you are, Livy! Could kill someone if they fell!"

At Olivia's insistence, Monty divested himself of

Nigel's greatcoat and she donned it, then stepped out onto the porch. In a moment she returned, wide-eyed.

"I apologize, Monty!" she exclaimed. "You weren't exaggerating at all! If anything, they are longer than you said!"

Monty nodded. "Told you. Best stay in the house for now. No place to go, at any rate. Might as well go play billiards with the Terrors after breakfast."

Olivia glanced at him mischievously. "Just think, Monty. Now that it has stopped snowing, you will soon be able to take them out in your curricle again."

For a moment Monty paled, but then reason asserted itself. He shook his head. "Won't be cleared off enough for days," he said. "And even then, won't go out in the curricle. Not made for this kind of weather."

Having settled his mind about that, he retired to have his breakfast, and Elise and Olivia joined him.

"How cozy this is," said Olivia comfortably, "having chocolate and toast while it is so cold outside."

"Was it not just as cozy yesterday morning and the morning before that?" inquired her sister.

Olivia shook her head. "Then we were trapped. Being trapped is *not* cozy. Today I know that soon we will be able to go about our business just as we please."

Monty brightened visibly. "Able to go home and wear my own rig!"

"Monty, you are most ungrateful," complained Nigel, strolling into the room. "Have I not supplied you with everything you need? Indeed, the *best* of everything?"

His brother nodded. "Very kind," he said. "Not the point. Wish to wear my own rig."

"Naturally you do," replied Elise. "We will all be able to go about our proper business now."

"And your proper business will be shopping for your bridal regalia, will it not, cousin?" inquired Nigel as Walter Belvedere appeared and made his way to the sideboard.

Elise was uncomfortably aware of Belvedere's presence in the room as she answered, feeling every inch the hypocrite because she did not simply state that she was not getting married. Nonetheless, she knew that she should not do so until she had heard from her father.

"Not just at first, Nigel. As I said the other day, Olivia and I have a few other things that we would like to do before we get down to serious business. As soon as the weather allows, we will make the most of our time here in town."

Mr. Belvedere sat down across from her, and she could feel him studying her. That made her uneasy, and then she was annoyed with herself—and still more annoyed with him—for feeling that way.

Fortunately the others came in together just then and the conversation became general. She was able to relax and listen to the flow of words around her. She began to feel that Olivia was correct; it was very cozy to be having a comfortable breakfast on an icy morning—particularly with the prospect of getting out once again.

A sudden outbreak of screams and laughter broke out above them—not just the sound of one or two voices, but of a mob. The pounding of feet—sounding like a herd suddenly startled by a predator and fleeing to safety—rocked the household. The diners stared at one another.

"What in the name of heaven—" began Nigel, looking up at the chandelier, which was rocking dangerously.

They waited for a moment, but the upheaval showed no sign of abating. Together, they rose from their half-eaten breakfasts and started toward the stairway. Only Mr. Belvedere and Monty remained at their places, still calmly drinking their coffee.

"Rocks," observed Monty astutely. "Knew it wouldn't be long before they were at it again."

Beavers, who had also rushed in the direction of the outbreak, tersely informed Ravinia of the situation when she arrived upstairs.

"It appears, madam, that Master Reginald and Master Theodore climbed out on the roof and formed quite a large number of snowballs. Aside from throwing them at Miss Marjorie and Master Lionel and their cousins, they also attacked the upstairs maids and Miss Dawson."

"Did they indeed?" inquired Ravinia, her eyes glittering. "And have they disposed of all their ammunition?"

"I believe that they have, ma'am—unless they venture farther out on the roof than they have gone thus far."

Ravinia started toward the door to the schoolroom, to which they had retreated after completing their raid.

"Mama-in-law, let me talk to them," pleaded Lucy, trying to move ahead of her.

"I believe not, Lucy," she replied. "They may be your sons, but they have overset *my* household, and I will deal with them. You may speak with them afterward."

Her tone brooked no interference, so Lucy moved reluctantly away as her mother-in-law entered the room and closed the door behind her. Those standing in the passageway listened with interest, but they could hear only the low murmur of Ravinia's voice, punctuated by an occasional brief remark from one of the boys. There was no arguing.

Ravinia opened the door and spoke to her daughter-in-law. "Lucy, you need to provide your sons with the warmest clothes they have. I will have Dawson check the attic for any old winter clothing that belonged to my children as well. In thirty minutes they are to report to me downstairs, prepared to go outdoors."

"Outdoors?" gasped Lucy. "In this cold?"

Ravinia nodded. "They have been scrambling about

on the roof in their shirtsleeves and have spent their time with their hands in the snow. I am going to provide them with the opportunity to apply that energy to a goal that is helpful instead of harmful."

"What are they going to do?" Lucy asked.

"They will work under the guidance of Davis and Hughes to clear the area in front of our steps and to begin work on clearing the areaway of snow as well."

"But they are gentlemen's sons!" their mother protested.

"Then they should behave as gentlemen," replied Ravinia shortly, walking by the others and going in search of Dawson.

"Should have known better," said Monty when the others filed back into the dining room and Elise told him what had happened.

"Indeed they should have," agreed Sally. "They must have known Mama would not let them get by with it. They soaked my children and left puddles all over the upstairs—even Bangs was hiding under one of the beds with his fur wet."

"Well, Reggie and Theo will have time enough to mull over their sins," said their father. "I couldn't have thought of a better punishment myself."

After breakfast, the cleared area in front of Ravinia's home became crowded, for everyone wanted to come out to inspect progress. The workers had indeed made inroads in the waves of snow, and two huge banks as high as the heads of the adults flanked both sides of the porch and steps. The two boys, far from appearing either exhausted or cowed, were obviously reveling in their work.

"Aunt Ravinia certainly found an excellent channel for all of that boyish energy," remarked Elise to Monty, as they stood shivering and marveling at the industry of the workers. "At this rate, they could work their way down the entire side of the square by sunset. Then Aunt will have to think of something else to occupy them."

"Skating," responded Monty. "That would do the trick."

"Skating? Do you mean ice skating, Monty?" she asked. "Where could they go?"

"Daresay the Serpentine has frozen over. Certain of it, as a matter of fact. Have a good little walk over there, skate in the afternoon, wear 'em down to a thread so there's no mischief left in 'em."

"What a very good idea, Monty!" she said admiringly. "I shouldn't imagine that you'd be able to do that today, though."

He shook his head in agreement and they stared about them at the vast expanse of snow. It would take a goodly amount of work just to provide narrow walkways so that people could move beyond their own homes. London had come to a virtual standstill.

"Look!" said Elise, pointing down the street. Ravinia's house occupied most of this side of the square, so they were the only ones to be seen outside, but at the far corner two sweeps had appeared, working diligently. Elise and Monty stood for a while, watching them work, but the cold was too intense for them to remain out for long periods of time, and they moved back inside to thaw by the fire. Even the boys, who had been told they must work all morning, were commanded to come in for periodic warm-ups.

After Elise had removed her wraps, she stopped in the library for a moment to return a book she had borrowed from the shelf there. Mr. Belvedere had stacked his notes neatly and was sitting with the notebook in front of him.

"And so, Miss MacGregor, will you be purchasing your bride clothes and then going directly home to be married?" he asked her abruptly.

Thrown off-guard by his unexpected question, Elise

said, "That is the plan, Mr. Belvedere." At least that much was true, she thought.

"And does your fiancé treat you as Mr. Gray does?" he inquired.

Elise thought about the contrast between the two for a moment and very nearly laughed aloud. Instead, she merely shook her head. "They are very different."

"That could be a good thing, Miss MacGregor," he replied.

"Why do you say that?" she demanded. "And why are you so very interested in my affairs?"

"I say that because it is true!" he responded sharply, ignoring her last question. "I loathe pretense and preening, so if the man you are to marry is so very different from your Mr. Gray, you will very likely be better off."

Before she could respond to this renewed attack upon James Gray, he pulled a paper from his sheaf of notes and pointed at it. "Look at this, Miss MacGregor!"

Curious despite her anger, Elise walked over to the table. He had pulled out the sheet that he had shown her earlier, with the three rings sketched upon it. He pointed to the one with the two hands clasped engraved upon it.

"That is a betrothal ring, Miss MacGregor—" he began, but Elise interrupted.

"Yes, you have shown me this, Mr. Belvedere, and it is all very interesting, but I do not need to see it again."

He ignored her protest and continued with his thought. "—and you will notice that the two hands are clasped together, symbolic, of course, of the closeness of the bond."

She glared at him impatiently. "Yes, I do understand that, Mr. Belvedere. Regardless of what you may think, I am not a simpleton!"

"I do not think you a simpleton at all, ma'am," he said gravely, "but I do believe that you are not thinking clearly. I believe that you should take the measure of Mr. Gray and the measure of your fiancé, and then make your decision. If you need to change it, do so—but think carefully. Do not let your emotions run away with you."

Elise stared at him. Never in her life had anyone accused her of allowing her emotions to run away with her. It had always been the reverse, as it was when Livy accused her of making her decision to marry Mr. Westbrook with no emotion at all.

For a moment she was speechless, but then she gathered her wits and remembered that he had ignored her other question.

"You may be assured, sir, that I will make the wisest decision of which I am capable. And I do appreciate your concern for my welfare, of course," she added, her voice misleadingly sweet.

He nodded briefly to acknowledge her thanks, but pulled up sharply with her next comment.

"But what puzzles me, Mr. Belvedere, is why you—who have no interest in anyone or anything other than the ancients—have taken such an interest in my personal affairs?"

She looked up at him with as mild an expression as she could manage, and it was only with great restraint that she could keep from smiling. He had not been prepared for her question.

He paused a moment, then turned away and slipped the page back into its proper place in the stack of notes and closed the box that held the original notebook. Finally he turned back to her, and she was startled by the intensity of his gaze.

"I would prefer, ma'am, that you not waste yourself," he replied. "You need to think carefully. As I told you earlier, you should ask young Gray if he knows of your engagement."

"I suppose you are referring to his compliment to me,

which you most unchivalrously referred to as 'false coin'!" she retorted. "I would remind you, sir, that you yourself said much the same thing to me just the other evening!"

To her surprise, his face showed a slight tinge of color high on the cheekbones, but he continued to look into her eyes. "I remember that very well, Miss MacGregor—but the difference is that I do not deal in false coin. I say what I mean."

Elise, fully prepared to do battle for Mr. Gray's honor, had just opened her mouth to speak when she inexplicably found herself folded within Mr. Belvedere's arms.

"Nor do I require a kissing bough!" he announced, and pressed his lips to hers. Elise stiffened and prepared to resist, but she suddenly realized that she did not wish to. The warmth she felt rushing through her and the tingling sensation, as though she had long been cold and had suddenly come to the fire's warmth, were completely unfamiliar and completely overwhelming. After a moment, she slipped her arms around his neck and returned his kiss warmly.

Monty, who had been searching for Elise, strolled by the library just then. Startled, he stood there for a moment, staring at the couple. Suddenly mindful of his manners, he quietly shut the library door and stood there thinking.

Important problems did not often come Monty's way, and whenever they did, he normally managed to avoid them very neatly. This time, however, he was trapped. He felt a strong affection for his cousins, and he could see that Elise had a problem. Livy had told him she had no affection for her fiancé, and Monty himself had seen the flirtation with James Gray, although it had not troubled him. This business with Belvedere, though, looked to be more serious.

Back in the library, the kiss had ended, and the two

participants stared into each other's eyes. It would have been difficult to say which one was the more startled.

Finally Mr. Belvedere bowed briefly to her and said in a low voice, "I beg your pardon, ma'am," just as though he had stepped on her foot or bumped into her on the street.

He gathered up his notes swiftly and bowed once more. "I assure you, Miss MacGregor, that I shall be leaving almost immediately. You will not be troubled by me again."

He moved swiftly to the library door, opened it, and then shut it softly behind him. Elise stood there, rooted to the spot.

She had been so clearheaded, so sensible, so certain of what she would do. She would marry Robert Westbrook. Then she had come to London and met James Gray and become equally certain that she should not marry Robert Westbrook. Now she had allowed Mr. Belvedere, of all people, to kiss her—and what was worse, she had returned the kiss!

What had come over her? How had she changed so much in a fortnight's time?

Fourteen

To Elise's relief, Mr. Belvedere was as good as his word. She did not have to see him again. By the time they assembled for dinner that evening, he had gone.

Monty had inquired casually where he was, and Ravinia told them that he had come to the morning room to thank her for allowing him to see the notebook and for their hospitality during the storm, then left for his parents' home. She did not add how pleased she was by the mere fact that he had come in to thank her and to say good-bye. Such a gesture was a giant step in the social graces for Walter Belvedere. She was exceedingly pleased with the way things had gone during his visit, and she had been thinking about the most effective way to continue his education.

"Do you mean he's walked home through all this mess?" demanded Nigel, glancing fastidiously at his own immaculate breeches and slippers. "He will be a wreck."

Ravinia nodded. "No doubt that is true, but he did not seem to see it as any particular problem," she observed.

"That's because he's mad as a hatter," replied Nigel.

"Don't know about that," demurred Monty, darting a glance at Elise. "Seems a good enough sort of chap. Surprised me. Not what I expected."

"Well, I suppose that's true enough," conceded Nigel.

"And I have only to look round the table to know that he's an observant chap," said Charles, one eyebrow raised. "He had us properly pegged the second time he sat down to breakfast with us."

At this, the others—with the natural exception of Lucy—dissolved into laughter.

Sally, wiping her eyes, said, "Here we were, all thinking how odd a fish he was, and he was sitting there watching us and thinking the very same thing. He has a very good eye for character."

"It is rather nice to be able to laugh at oneself," agreed Nigel, "although naturally it is much more comfortable to laugh at others."

The conversation passed on to other things, but Monty was satisfied that he had contributed his mite on behalf of Belvedere. He *did* rather like him, odd fish or not, and if Elise did, too—well, he would simply have to see what he could do about the situation.

To everyone's relief, they were soon able to get out of the house. They could not go too far, and many of the shops were either closed or too difficult to reach as yet, but they could at least get some fresh air—and they could go skating! Monty was quite right; the Serpentine, like virtually every other body of water in the area, had frozen over.

"Heard the Thames is freezing over, too," he observed, after one of his forays into the outside world. "Huge chunks of ice floating out there since the storm. Cracked up against each other and made a fearful row. Said it sounded like cannon fire. Sticking together and freezing over now."

"How extraordinary!" said Sally. "If the river really does freeze over, perhaps there'll be another Frost Fair!"

Olivia stared at her. "A Frost Fair? What do you mean, Sally?"

"There hasn't been one in decades, for the Thames

has to freeze over quite firmly in order for it to work. But when it does, they set up booths and tents like a regular fair, and everybody goes!"

"In all this cold?" demanded Olivia.

"Well, aren't you about to go skating?" asked Sally reasonably. "And won't that be outside in the cold?"

Olivia nodded. "But we will be moving, which will make us warmer, and there will be fires, too." She thought about it a moment. "And of course we will have our fur-lined cloaks and muffs, too!"

Ravinia had instructed Dawson to scour the attic and find what was needed to outfit the family warmly. Elise and Olivia had received old-fashioned velvet cloaks, both lined with fur, that Ravinia's mother, who had been short like the two girls, had worn many years ago.

"Yes," nodded Elise, "we'll be in no danger from the cold with those—and we will, of course, also be stunningly elegant!"

"Naturally," responded Olivia, smiling. Then she lowered her voice and whispered across Monty, who was sitting beside her, to her sister, "Everything will be perfect, if only Mr. Townsend will stay far away."

As soon as there were adequate pathways through the snow, James Gray and Arthur Townsend had come to call, assuring the family that they had come to inquire about their welfare after the storm and to see if they might be of some assistance. Mr. Gray was warmly received and Mr. Townsend scarcely tolerated. Unfortunately, Arthur Townsend seemed absolutely impervious to snubs, and good breeding would not allow Olivia to tell him precisely how much he annoyed her. Elise had done her best to intercede, and when Mr. Gray was present, they had both engaged Olivia in conversation and tried to keep Mr. Townsend from hedging her in with compliments and attentions.

"See what I can do about Townsend," said Monty suddenly. "Have an idea."

Olivia flung her arms around his neck and hugged him. "You are the best of cousins!" she exclaimed.

Monty flushed to the roots of his hair, and Nigel said, "I had thought that I was. I am quite crushed."

Olivia started to explain to him, but he held up his hand and said, "If it has anything to do with my going out to spend time in this weather, my brother is very welcome to remain the best of cousins. I relinquish my title to him gladly for the sake of the fire."

"Should come skating with us, Nigel," Monty urged, but Nigel was immovable and, catlike, remained by the fire.

Before they left for their outing to the Serpentine that afternoon, Monty stopped in Curzon Street to call upon Walter Belvedere. Taken by surprise, Belvedere left his books and went down to the drawing room, where Monty was waiting.

"Longfellow," he said, bowing. "Is there something I can do for you?"

Grateful for this opening, Monty nodded and plunged in. "Just it. Need some help for my cousin."

"For Miss MacGregor?" he asked, frowning. "What seems to be the problem?"

"Not Elise," said Monty. "Olivia. Young Townsend always showering her with attention. Livy's too young for it—not out yet. Don't know how to handle him."

"But what does that have to do with me?" he asked, growing more and more puzzled.

"Going skating on the Serpentine this afternoon," said Monty desperately. "Thought you might help. Come along and keep close by Livy so he won't bother her."

"Why don't you do that yourself?" asked Belvedere reasonably.

Monty shook his head. "Got the Terrors to watch, and Marjorie. Too much to do."

Belvedere allowed himself a smile as he pictured this scene. "You've bitten off rather more than you can chew, haven't you, Longfellow?"

Monty grimaced. "Don't I know it? Threatened 'em within an inch of their lives if they so much as think about making a snowball."

His prey regarded him thoughtfully, and Monty persevered.

"Come now, Belvedere, be a good chap. Can't leave the girl unprotected." Then, having a sudden flash of inspiration, he added, "Thought you might wish to be back again with the other odd ones."

To his relief, Belvedere laughed and, after a moment, nodded. "I'll just be a moment, Longfellow. Let me find something a little warmer to wear."

A few minutes later the footman was about to open the door for the two of them to leave the house when Belvedere's parents came down the stairs.

"Why, good day, Mr. Longfellow," said Muriel Belvedere, surprised at the sight of the visitor. "Did you come to bring me a message from your mother?"

Monty bowed, but before he could speak, Walter Belvedere replied, "He came to call for me, Mother. We're going out."

"Really?" said his mother, truly startled now. Walter never went out with anyone. "Where are you going?"

Her son glanced over his shoulder just as the door was closing behind them. "Skating," he replied.

Muriel Belvedere clutched her husband's arm. "Freddie! Isn't it marvelous? Walter has made a *friend!*"

* * *

The scene at the Serpentine was a delightful whirl of color and movement. The sweepers had cleared a number of places on the ice—circles, squares, and rectangles had appeared among mountains of snow—and skaters were occupying all of them. Green Park and the Canal were also the scene of skating frolic, but the Serpentine in Hyde Park drew a more elegant clientele. Elise and Olivia were by no means the only ladies there in fur-lined cloaks. Olivia whispered to her sister that she was beginning to feel like a dowd when a particularly lovely woman, covered from head to heel in ermine, skated gracefully by on the arm of a man in the uniform of a hussar.

Monty had his own skates, but he stopped at the booth of an enterprising young man who was offering skates for hire. The gentlemen strapped on their own skates, fitting the leather straps over their boots, and then knelt to help the ladies take care of theirs. Soon they all took the ice, including Reginald and Theodore, who treated the ice as though it were a race track, whipping around the outside of the rectangle as fast as they could go, their scarves snapping in the wind.

"Might have to find a space where they can be alone," commented Monty, watching them. "Dangerous."

Elise laughed. "Well, until they run someone down, let's just enjoy ourselves and skate, Monty."

Monty looked undecided, his eyes on the boys speeding across the ice, but he gave in to her request and took Marjorie by the hand as James Gray offered Elise his arm. Together the four of them glided out into the crowd, followed by Olivia and Walter Belvedere, and finally by Arthur Townsend.

Lionel had a cold, and Sally had decided that it was too cold for her children, so they had stayed at home, promising to keep Nigel company by the fire. The last thing that Elise had seen as she left her aunt's house was

Nigel's hunted expression, and the last thing she had heard had been Sally's laughter.

"Told him he should come skating," said Monty smugly, as the footman closed the door behind them.

Elise had made no comment when Monty called for them with Walter Belvedere in tow. Although she had half expected him to make some sort of overture to her, at least more than the bow and brief greeting he accorded her, she had understood the reason for his presence once Monty announced that Belvedere had been kind enough to offer to teach Olivia to skate.

Olivia had opened her mouth to respond indignantly that she had doubtless had occasion to skate as frequently as had Mr. Belvedere and Monty, but Monty caught her eye and shook his head slightly, raising his eyes and glancing in Townsend's direction.

"I should be most happy to teach you, Miss Olivia," Townsend had said eagerly. "Pray give me the pleasure."

Olivia had smiled gently. "Thank you, sir," she replied, "but since Mr. Belvedere has been so kind as to make a special trip to help me, I feel I should allow him to do so."

She had taken Belvedere's arm, and he had escorted her to the park, just as James Gray had escorted Elise, and Monty had escorted Marjorie. The Terrors ranged about them, sometimes ahead of them, sometimes behind, sometimes rushing at them from the side, having run round a bank of snow and discovered another side entrance to the main path that had been cleared for pedestrians.

As Elise glided around the rink, enjoying the fragrance of roasting chestnuts from a nearby stand, she glanced up at the face of her partner. Such clearly chiseled features, she thought, and such an alert, merry countenance! She was indeed a fortunate young woman to be skating with so charming a man.

For a moment she thought of putting Mr. Belvedere's question to him and discovering then and there if he knew of her engagement, but she decided against it. Why spoil a lovely afternoon by thinking about Robert Westbrook? Besides, she would like to be able to tell him that she had broken that engagement at the same time she asked him if he knew of it. There would be too much awkwardness otherwise. Pleased with her decision, she gave herself up to the pleasures of the afternoon.

They paused for a moment so that Mr. Gray could tighten the strap of his skate, and as he rose from the ice and once more offered her his arm, he observed, "Perhaps we should skate beside your sister. My heart goes out to her for being obliged to skate with Belvedere, and I see that Townsend is closing in on her other side."

Elise could see that it was true. Belvedere was Livy's escort, but Townsend refused to be deterred, having attached himself like a burr to her unprotected side.

"Yes," she responded. "We most certainly should. Although I am certain that there is no problem with having Mr. Belvedere as a partner, since we got to know him rather better during the storm. I promised our father that I would keep her from being bothered by Mr. Townsend's attentions."

Accordingly, they sped up, and when they were behind the three, James Gray said, "Belvedere, could I have a word with you?"

Walter Belvedere slowed and dropped back, and as he did so, Gray moved smoothly into place beside Olivia, linking his arm through hers and locking her between them. "I thought perhaps we might skate as a fivesome."

This naturally left Mr. Townsend to take Elise's free arm, which he reluctantly did, seeing that his place beside Olivia was gone.

"Just so long as you are not planning a game of Crack the Whip, Gray," Belvedere said gravely.

The young man laughed. "No, I promise you that, Belvedere. That would be much too dangerous in such a crowded space."

And the rectangle carved from the snow in which they were skating was certainly crowded. Most of the skaters were adults, all fashionably dressed, and a handful of children flitted among them, including Reginald and Theodore. They were still skating rapidly, completing three circuits of the rink for every one that the adults and Marjorie completed. On their last time past their companions, Reginald had attempted to execute a brief jump, lost his balance, and gone flying into the bank of snow that surrounded the rink.

"I hope that the boys realize that Crack the Whip would be too dangerous," said Elise. "That would be all we would need in such cramped quarters."

To their dismay, however, it appeared that flying into the snowbank had given them an idea. It was not long until they saw that the boys had joined forces with four other youngsters. They were all holding hands and gathering speed as they moved around the perimeter of the rink. Since there was not enough space for them to skate side by side as they were building their speed, Reginald led the way while the others, still holding hands, fell in behind him. At the first break among the skaters, the other boys shot alongside Reginald, who promptly "cracked the whip." He stopped abruptly and swung round, sending the rest of the line spinning back among the other skaters.

Some managed to move quickly enough to avoid any encounter, but two ladies and a gentleman were overset, and for the moment the rink became a scene of chaos. Ladies shrieked, gentlemen cursed, and the boys, scrambling to their feet, ran. Running on metal blades was no easy task, but fear propelled them.

Elise and her party had stopped to help those who

had been overset, and were relieved to see that none of them had been hurt, although they had been seriously ruffled in spirit. Marjorie skated up and took Elise's hand as she stood beside one of the ladies, and Elise looked round for her cousin.

"Where is Monty?" she asked Marjorie. "I thought that he was with you."

"He was," she replied, "until the accident." She pointed into the distance. "He is chasing Reggie and Theo."

"Did he take off his skates?" Elise demanded, noticing that Mr. Belvedere was listening with some interest.

Marjorie shook her head. "He said that if the Terrors could do it, he could, too, and then he told me to skate over to you."

Suddenly they heard a flurry of excitement behind them, and the boys, still going at a dead run, roared over the top of the snow bank that edged their particular section of the Serpentine. The surface of the snow had frozen quite firmly so that the boys did not sink at all as they ran, but angling down from the snowbank and hitting the ice running provided a navigational problem. The other skaters, seeing them coming again, scattered to the safety of the sides as the boys raced down the middle.

To her astonishment, Monty was just behind them, and his long legs and even gait were providing him with the advantage. When his blades hit the ice, he struck out with a long, gliding step and moved rapidly down the clear section of the rink. His long arms caught the boys by the collar, one in each of his hands, just before they left the ice and began the race up the opposite snowbank.

A smattering of applause and a few shouted suggestions as to their fate greeted their capture. Keeping them firmly in hand, Monty skated over to join the rest of the group.

"Knew it!" he said grimly. "Knew I shouldn't have brought them!"

"But we're sorry, Uncle Monty," Reginald said plaintively. "We won't do it again."

"Know you won't," replied Monty. "Taking you home after you make your apologies."

Despite Reginald's pleas—Theo wisely said nothing—Monty marched them over to apologize to their victims, told them to remove their skates, and escorted them directly home, leaving Marjorie to skate with Elise and Olivia.

After Monty left, they skated in threes. Elise was not certain just how it came to pass, but Mr. Belvedere skated with Olivia and Marjorie, while she skated with Mr. Gray and Mr. Townsend. She was not best pleased, for it seemed to her that both of the gentlemen with her were still centering their attention upon Olivia. Mr. Townsend, naturally, longed to be by her side, and Mr. Gray was still disturbed that she had been forced to partner with Walter Belvedere.

All things considered, she was very grateful when the others decided that it was time to leave. It was already growing dark, the early gray twilight of a winter evening, and the cold was growing more intense. Marjorie was clearly exhausted, and Mr. Belvedere, to Elise's amazement, swept the child into his arms and carried her home.

When they reached Darlington Square, Marjorie was bundled upstairs to the nursery, and the rest of the group was regaled with hot chocolate and brandy by Nigel, who was still planted snugly by the fireside in the drawing room.

"Where are the Terrors and Monty?" inquired Elise.

"Monty confined them to the schoolroom and did the

most horrible thing to them that he could think of. He is making them read a history lesson—I believe he chose Agincourt—and he told them he would quiz them afterward."

Here he paused and grinned at his interested listeners, who were surprised by Monty's foray into the books he dreaded. "Of course, Monty didn't realize until it was too late for him to back out of it that he would have to read about it, too. And so he is presently in the library, suffering over his lesson."

"Poor Monty," laughed Elise, "those boys are certainly giving him a run for his money." She thought about it a moment, then added, "Of course, it is very good of him to spend time with them, for Charles and Lucy appear to pay little enough attention to them."

Nigel nodded. "Charles discovered that he could make it to his club, where there are more up-to-date newspapers, and Lucy has stayed in her room today—not that I am complaining about that, you understand," he added hastily.

Ravinia entered at this point and smiled to see that Belvedere was still a part of the group. "Gentlemen," she said, "we would be delighted if you could stay for dinner with us tonight. It will be just the family, of course, but it is Twelfth Night, so there will at least be a few games and the children's Twelfth Night cakes. Do say that you will dine with us."

"I would be delighted, ma'am," said Mr. Townsend, bowing with alacrity. Olivia sighed and glanced at her sister.

"As would I," added James Gray, smiling in the direction of the sofa where Elise and Olivia were seated.

"And you, Mr. Belvedere," said Ravinia, "will you join us as well?"

Belvedere shook his head and started to speak, but

Monty, standing in the doorway, interrupted. "O' course he will," he said.

When Belvedere looked up in surprise, Monty nodded at him vigorously. "Promised. Don't you recall? Said you would help me with a little matter." Here he glanced significantly toward Olivia.

Mr. Belvedere's lips twisted slightly at Monty's attempts at subtlety, but he nodded briefly and replied, "Indeed I do. It's good of you to remind me."

Then he bowed to Ravinia and added, "I would be happy to join you for dinner, ma'am," he said.

Monty smiled, satisfied, and Ravinia rang for Beavers to inform Cook that there would be three more for dinner.

Elise, who had followed the curious exchange between her cousin and Belvedere, looked at them with puzzlement. She understood that Monty had convinced Walter Belvedere to help protect Olivia from the attentions of young Townsend, but it seemed most unlike him to have agreed to do such a thing—and still more unlike him to agree to stay even longer. She watched him as he walked over to the sofa where they were seated, and he promptly engaged Olivia in conversation.

Elise frowned. She would have been much happier if Mr. Belvedere had decided to leave.

Fifteen

Dinner was not a formal affair, since their guests could scarcely plow home through the snow and come back again in the proper dress. Elise and Olivia went to their chamber to repair the effects of the afternoon, and Monty went to the schoolroom, his head full of St. Crispin's Day and Henry V, to batter the Terrors with questions.

"I was very surprised to see Mr. Belvedere today," said Olivia, "but I was never more grateful to have someone walk with me. He certainly helped to keep Arthur Townsend at bay."

"Mr. Gray did his best to be of assistance, too," replied Elise. In fact, it had seemed to her that he had been of far too much assistance, although she could not, naturally, say so.

"Yes, he did," agreed Olivia thoughtfully. "He really is a most charming man—and striking to look at as well. It is such a pleasant thing when men *are* handsome."

Elise smiled. "Being decorative, whether male or female, seems always to be helpful. It is a pity that not all of us can be either handsome or beautiful."

"Why do you speak of 'us' when you say that? Don't try to deny that you are very attractive, Elise," scolded her sister, "for you know very well that you would be fibbing if you did so."

Elise did not reply, but continued to comb her hair,

looking at the pearl combs and wondering if she dared
to wear them tonight.

"Mr. Belvedere is not dashing and handsome like Mr.
Gray," continued Olivia dreamily, "but he is a much
more enjoyable companion than I would have thought
him. It was very kind of him to come along to protect
me, don't you think?"

"Certainly it was," replied Elise, smoothing her hair
and tucking in the pearl combs. They would look very
well with the blue merino she was wearing down to dinner—not too formal, not too showy. She did not allow
herself to consider just why she had chosen to wear
them, only that she wished to do so. "I believe that you
may thank Monty for that. Recall that's why he said that
you needed help skating. It was to protect you from Mr.
Townsend."

"That's true," said Olivia, thinking it over, "but Mr.
Belvedere most certainly did not have to come. I daresay
he would never have thought of coming skating himself,
and yet he put himself to all that trouble. It was very
chivalrous of him."

"Yes—yes, it was," agreed Elise, working to maintain a
disinterested tone. She had had the same thought herself. Just why had he chosen to be so chivalrous, she
wondered. She had seen little enough of such behavior
from him herself.

As they went down to the drawing room, they were
joined on the stairs by Monty, trailed by the Terrors, who
had apparently outdone themselves in answering the
questions put to them about Agincourt. They were not
to be allowed to take dinner with the adults, but they
would, in honor of the occasion, be allowed to join them
for games and the Twelfth Night cakes afterward. At the
moment they apparently fancied themselves a formal escort for their mentor.

"The cakes are the best part, at any rate!" said Theo,

disappearing in the direction of the billiards room when they reached the first floor.

"I'm pleased to see that you survived, Monty," drawled Nigel when they entered the drawing room. "I had thought of going up and delivering Henry's speech before going into battle, but it was too much of an exertion. I stayed here by the fire."

"Just as well," said Monty. "Don't want to stir them up any more than can be avoided."

"I am overcome that you think my delivery could have stirred them up," replied his brother, mildly surprised, both by the unexpected tribute and by the equally unexpected revelation that Monty was aware that Henry's speech was supposed to stir the audience.

"Not that," returned Monty frankly. "Been mimicking you. Had to threaten 'em to make them stop it."

"Mimicking *me?*" demanded Nigel, outraged. "I should hope you did threaten them! Did you tell them you would give them another quiz?"

Monty shook his head. "Wouldn't have done it. Told 'em they were still small enough to be sweeps." He smiled with satisfaction. "Did the trick. Scared the liver out of 'em."

The life of chimney sweeps was miserable and quite often brief. The unfortunate children were made to crawl into chimneys to clean them, and, if they survived, their health often failed.

"Monty!" said Lucy sternly. She had not been attending to the entire conversation, but she had heard the latter portion. "What a dreadful thing to tell them! You have probably inflicted emotional wounds on those poor boys!"

"Nothing to mine," returned Monty, unrepentant. "Dashed fortunate not to have physical wounds, too. Ran over people on the ice!"

Elise glanced at Mr. Belvedere, who had been following the exchange idly. "Perhaps you would like to take Reginald and Theodore home with you, sir," she said in a low voice. "They would enliven it."

"I had suspected, Miss MacGregor, that you hold me in dislike, but I had no notion that it ran so deep," he returned in a disinterested voice.

Elise chuckled. "Monty would be perfectly willing to share his charges, I assure you."

"Not for the world would I attempt to intrude upon that touching relationship between uncle and nephew," he answered her gravely. "I hold it sacred."

Ravinia, standing close enough to overhear, was astonished. This was Walter Belvedere, who never bothered to string more than three words together to speak to anyone—if, indeed, he bothered to speak at all! How very far he had come in such a very short time. She had been surprised to learn that Monty had sought his company, but when she understood the reason for it—assisting Olivia, for Monty had mentioned nothing of seeing Elise and Belvedere—she realized that her son had an astuteness that she had not credited him for. She knew that Monty was a kindhearted soul, but now she knew him to be, as he put it, "awake on all counts."

Mr. Gray escorted Elise in to dinner but, as it had been on other occasions, the conversation was general and lively.

"I heard an interesting bit of news at the club," Charles announced. "Seems that the Thames has finally frozen over from Blackfriars to London Bridge. Looks as though we're about to have a frolic on the ice."

Sally clapped her hands together. "A frost fair!" she exclaimed. "We shall all go!"

"But will it be safe?" asked Elise anxiously. "Isn't there a great danger in going out on the river? What if it simply appears to be frozen?"

"I understand that seventy people walked back and

forth across it today with no difficulty," said Edward. "If it hadn't been so cold, I might have been tempted to go down there and watch them from the bridge."

"Send the Terrors to check the ice," said Monty. "Good use for them."

Lucy shot him an outraged look, but the conversation continued before she could say anything.

"A frost fair!" shuddered Nigel. "How delightful! You can be entertained while you are freezing to death!"

"Don't be such a stick, Nigel! It will be great fun!" said Olivia.

"Your Romans would have had a terrible time in a blizzard like this, Belvedere," said Nigel, not wishing for his cousin to begin trying to convince him to attend. "They would probably all be huddled around their fires or lie frozen in the snow."

"Rather like us," observed Charles, "particularly you, Nigel. Preventing you from huddling over that fire would require an act of God."

"Actually, the Romans in some of the villas would have been better off than we are," replied Belvedere. "Many of them had central heating systems."

"Central heating?" demanded Monty, his eyes wide. "How do you mean?"

"Stone channels ran under the tile floors, directing the heat from a central fire chamber to all the parts of the house, warming it from below," explained Belvedere.

"And that was fifteen hundred years ago," observed Elise. "We seem to have gone downhill since then."

Belvedere nodded. "They were a formidable force— in many ways."

"Had no idea they did anything useful," sighed Monty. "Should have paid more attention to my books."

"You were not even aware that you *had* any books to attend to!" retorted Nigel.

"Who knows," said Belvedere idly, "at this very moment we may be having dinner just over such a villa—or perhaps the baths or a temple to Mithras." He watched with amusement as Monty cast a worried glance toward the floor, as though expecting such ruins suddenly to appear.

"Built over 'em, have we?" Monty asked uneasily.

Belvedere nodded. "Undoubtedly," he replied. "If we dug far enough and found such a villa, perhaps your brother would not be forced to huddle by the fire in cold such as this."

Satisfied that he had defended his interests adequately, he returned to his dinner, merely watching the others.

Arthur Townsend, feeling that it had been too long since he had paid some small tribute to Olivia, took advantage of the pause in conversation to say, "And if we had lived in the London of Roman times, I am certain that Miss Olivia would have been the chief ornament of the city—as would the other ladies here, of course," he added hastily, suddenly realizing his error.

Olivia looked slightly queasy, but Nigel inquired in an amused voice, "Just how would *all* the ladies present tonight have been the chief ornament, Townsend? If you say 'chief,' do you not mean one single superior being?"

As Mr. Townsend tried to extricate himself from his difficulty, James Gray took advantage of the moment to lean close to Elise and say in a lowered voice, "I see that you are once more wearing the pearl combs in your hair, Miss MacGregor. In the glow of the candles and the fire, it is difficult to tell which is more luminous—you or the pearls."

A sharp clearing of the throat caused Elise to glance up suspiciously. As she had suspected, Mr. Belvedere had raised his napkin to his lips and was looking directly at her, his eyes bright. Undoubtedly he had not missed a word.

Elise did not reply directly. She merely turned to Mr. Gray and smiled, in as luminous a manner as she could manage, hoping that Mr. Belvedere would see that she appreciated a gentlemanly compliment such as Mr. Gray's. For a moment she recalled Mr. Belvedere's much more direct tribute to her charms, and she glanced back over at him in spite of herself.

Walter Belvedere had turned his attention to Olivia, and was laughing with her over something, effectively closing Arthur Townsend out of the conversation for the moment.

When the ladies rose and retired to the drawing room, Elise settled herself with a copy of *Le Beau Monde*, but Olivia came to sit beside her, anxious to talk.

"It is difficult to tell who is more charming, isn't it, Elise?" she asked, her brow furrowed. "Of course we cannot include our cousins, and we must certainly exclude Arthur Townsend, who has no claim to charm, but it would be difficult to decide between Mr. Gray and Mr. Belvedere. I never would have thought there could be any comparison until just a day or two ago."

Elise had continued to turn the pages of the fashion journal idly, but here Olivia demanded, "What do you think, Elise?"

"About what?" she asked, closing the journal with a sigh. She was not going to be able to avoid the conversation.

"About who is more charming—Mr. Gray or Mr. Belvedere?" she repeated impatiently. "Weren't you attending to what I was saying? You are growing as difficult to talk to as Monty!"

"Well, allow me to think about it," said Elise. "They both are tall, both carry themselves well." She paused a moment in consideration. "I believe that Mr. Gray is more fashionable than Mr. Belvedere because he—"

Olivia slapped her sister's arm gently. "Don't be a

goose, Elise! That is not what I mean, and you know it! I am speaking of their manner!"

Elise was saved from having to answer by the advent of the children and the gentlemen. The children were in full cry, demanding their Twelfth Night cakes.

"They will arrive presently," said Ravinia calmly. "In the meantime, come in and be seated. I had promised Niles that he might choose the first game tonight."

Niles, having apparently already given the matter serious consideration, announced, "Hunt the Slipper!"

"And are you to be the Hunter, Niles?" asked Theodore, sighing. This was not one of his favorites.

Niles nodded emphatically and seated himself in the midst of the others.

"All right, then. Everyone form a circle around Niles," commanded Reginald, taking charge of the occasion.

The others did as they were bid, even the gentlemen. They formed a ragged circle, the ladies and gentlemen on sofas or chairs pulled close, the children and Sally on the carpet in the spaces between them. Bangs sat attentively next to Tillie, his ears pricked in anticipation.

"Here, Elise, let us have your shoe," said Monty, and Elise obligingly slipped off one of her heelless blue slippers and handed it to Reginald.

"Here it is then, Niles," said Reggie, showing his small cousin the shoe. "Now, close your eyes. Tightly, mind! No peeking!"

Niles put his hands tightly over his eyes and sat in the middle of the circle as the others chanted the lines: "Cobbler, cobbler, mend my shoe. Have it done by half past two." As they chanted, the slipper passed from person to person, all of them keeping their hands behind their backs.

When they reached the end of the rhyme, Niles opened his eyes and leaped to his feet, turning slowly and studying the faces of the people in the circle.

Intently he recited his lines, still looking from person to person. "Cobbler, cobbler, tell me true. Which of you has got my shoe?"

No one said anything, but Tillie and Nelson giggled nervously. Niles focused on his twin brother. "Do you have it?" he demanded of Nelson.

Nelson, giggling even harder, fell over on his back. "No!" he replied. "Not me!"

"You have two more guesses, Niles. Make them count," said Reginald.

Niles, his hands behind his back and looking as serious as a barrister at at the bar, studied the others, who looked back at him with expressions equally as serious. When he came to Olivia, she smiled at him, and he immediately guessed that she had it.

"Wrong!" said Reginald. "One more try, Niles, and then you must be the Hunter again."

Niles was beginning to look a little worried, and when his eyes met those of his mother, Sally glanced toward Theodore, who was looking very innocent.

"Theo's got it!" shouted Niles.

"Not fair!" shouted Theo. "Aunt Sally gave it away!"

He appeared prepared to protest, but then Monty caught his eye, and his complaints subsided.

And so the time passed, and Hunt the Slipper melted into a game of I Love My Love with an A as they awaited the arrival of the cakes.

"I love my love with a *k*, because she is so cruel," Theo chanted, and a general groan rolled through the room.

"Lucy, you must teach your children to spell," protested Nigel. "Even Monty can spell better than that!"

Lucy bristled. "Theo does perfectly well when he isn't playing some foolish game!" she retorted. "This is not a fair measure!"

Nigel shrugged. "You're next, Lucy," he reminded her.

"I am not participating," she replied shortly.

"Very well," he said. "Belvedere?"

There was a thoughtful pause, then Belvedere responded, "I love my love with an *l*, because she is so—luminous," he responded, glancing blandly at Elise, who flushed in irritation. A wicked reminder, she had no doubt, of Mr. Gray's compliment.

"A very interesting choice," said Ravinia. "And Elise? You are next."

"I love my love with an *m*, because he is so mannerless!" responded Elise, obviously irritated.

The others looked at her, startled by her answer, and Elise blushed. She had not meant to allow her annoyance to be made so clear.

"What has ruffled your feathers?" inquired Nigel.

"Nothing at all," she said hurriedly. "I simply couldn't think of anything else."

"You were certainly quick with your reply for someone who couldn't think of anything else," observed Olivia, looking at her sister curiously and wondering if she were thinking of Mr. Westbrook, who was notorious for his brusqueness.

Beavers entered at that moment, followed by two footmen bearing the refreshments.

"The cakes!" shouted the youngsters, eager for their treat.

"Well, prepare yourself, Elise," said Olivia. "Now we will discover our futures for the next year, for Aunt said that she had Cook bake one for all of us."

Baked in each of the little spice cakes was a silver charm to indicate symbolically what fate the person could expect for the coming year. Many people placed them in their Christmas puddings, but Ravinia preferred the Twelfth Night cakes.

"Chew slowly," Ravinia reminded the children. "We don't want anyone to swallow their future—or to break a tooth."

Theo found his first—a silver coin—and waved it in the air. "I'm going to be a wealthy man!" he shouted triumphantly. "What did you get, Reg?"

His brother frowned in disgust as he held up his. "A button!" he exclaimed indignantly.

"Well, there's a relief for us all," said Nigel. "You're going to remain a bachelor for the next year."

"Doesn't Bangs get one?" asked Tillie, holding hers, a tiny silver horseshoe for good luck.

"Indeed he does," answered her grandmother, nodding at Beavers. "Cook baked one especially for him, but you'd best take out his charm first so that he doesn't eat it."

Beavers brought over a small tray with a tiny cake on it. Tillie split it in two carefully as Bangs watched, his tail thumping anxiously.

"A bone!" she cried, holding it up the small trinket.

"And you know what that means, don't you?" asked Nelson. "Do you remember last year?"

Tillie shook her head. Last year was far too long ago for her. "It means that Bangs will have all the food he needs this year," explained her brother.

Tillie patted her pet happily as Bangs nibbled at his cake.

"Well, Livy?" asked Elise, smiling. "And what did you discover about the year that lies before you?"

Livy held up a silver ring, and everyone applauded, laughing.

"Ah, so Livy is to be a bride," said Nigel. "I should have thought that the ring would have been yours, Elise."

Elise glanced up quickly when he said this, but Mr. Gray did not seem to have heard it. He was still looking at Olivia and laughing at her dismay. Sally was holding up the cradle she had found in hers, and Edward was looking at the three children they already possessed.

Mr. Townsend held up the button from his cake in disappointment.

"I see that you won't be the groom, Townsend," said Charles, who was examining his silver book with interest. "And mine should have been a newspaper, not a book."

"What is your fortune, Mr. Gray?" inquired Elise.

"I believe that I shall be traveling," he said, holding up a tiny ship. "Who knows? Perhaps to the West Indies. And what did you discover, Miss MacGregor?"

"I shall have my wish," she replied smiling. Her charm was a tiny silver wishbone.

"And what shall you wish for?" he asked, his eyebrows lifted. "Have you decided?"

"That, I fear, is the difficulty," she said. "And since I only have one, I'd best make it count."

The others then gave their attention to Monty, who had just discovered his thimble and was complaining bitterly, but his pain was soon eclipsed by that of Nigel, who had discovered a silver cradle in his cake. A shout of laughter erupted, and Nigel proposed that the cook and Beavers should be let go immediately.

Under cover of the confusion, Mr. Belvedere murmured to Elise, "Such a pity that you did not find a pearl in yours, ma'am—so much more suitable."

"And what did you find in yours, Mr. Belvedere?" she asked, ignoring his comment.

"I fear I got Mr. Townsend's," he replied, showing her a small silver ring in the palm of his hand. He tucked it into the pocket of his waistcoat. "It is a fortunate thing that I am not a superstitious man. I should be driven to lock myself into my chamber and stay there until year's end."

As the evening closed, with laughter and promises to gather tomorrow to go down and inspect the Thames, Elise found herself wishing that she felt no twinge of superstition. She knew that the cakes with their charms were merely for the amusement of the children, but she found herself vaguely unsettled by it all.

She still held the tiny wishbone in her hand, and she still wondered just what she should be wishing. She had hoped to hear from her father very promptly. The mail was always efficient, and she knew that her father would not fail to reply when he received her letter. The storm, however, had put everything at sixes and sevens, and she had no notion when to expect a reply.

She could, of course, wish to hear from him immediately. Or she could wish for Mr. Gray to propose to her straightaway.

She laughed at herself. Why not simply wish that her future would be perfect? That she would marry a wonderful man who would delight her and who would think that she in turn was delightful? Why not wish to live happily ever after?

As she drifted off to sleep that night, she suddenly imagined herself once more in the arms of Walter Belvedere, his lips pressed against hers. She shook herself as a reminder that she had to be more judicious. Why she should have allowed him such a liberty—indeed, not simply allowed it, but enjoyed it—still seemed inexplicable to her. For a moment she thought of his eyes fixed intensely on hers as he told her she had no need of pearls—so strange to receive a compliment from such a man.

The last image that crossed her conscious mind, however, was the laughing face of James Gray. Such an agreeable, pleasant gentleman—how lovely it would be to spend her days with him.

She still held the wishbone tightly in her hand.

Sixteen

When Elise awoke in the morning, she was still clutching the wishbone firmly in her hand, and, so far as she could recollect, she had made no wish. She knew it was a pitiful superstition, and she would have been embarrassed had anyone—even the children—known that she was taking it at all seriously, but still she did not toss the charm away. She decided to keep it with her. If nothing else, it was a good luck talisman, she told herself. Some people carried a rabbit's foot. She carried a silver wishbone.

The morning was the brightest that they had seen since the storm, and Monty had already arrived for breakfast when she came down.

"Charles is bringing his carriage and I am taking Mama's," he told her. "Lucy doesn't want to go, and all the younger ones are staying home with Mama, but Charles will take the Terrors, along with Sally, Edward, and Townsend, and I will take you, Livy, Nigel, and Gray. And Belvedere—he said he'd come just today to help Livy."

He regarded her anxiously. "Wish to rearrange it, Elise?" he inquired. "Know you and Livy are the only females in the carriage, but Sally wished Edward to ride with her." He paused a moment, then added grimly, "Wanted Charles and Townsend to ride with the Terrors. Be good for 'em."

She shook her head. "No. That will be fine, Monty.

Papa would approve completely, since you and Nigel are along to be our chaperones. In fact, we quite prefer being with you."

Monty relaxed at her words, and smiled.

"I am surprised, though," she added lightly, "that you are *not* taking the Terrors with you, Monty. Perhaps Livy and I should offer to trade places with them?"

He shuddered. "Goose walking over my grave," he apologized. "Just saw that blacksmith from the city in my mind. Could have threaded me—and wanted to. Miracle I lived."

"Well, today they will be with their father, so all will be well," she assured him. "And I am looking forward to seeing the fair."

"Don't imagine they have much set up yet," he cautioned her. "Don't expect Scarborough Fair."

"Don't worry, Monty. I shall be delighted to see any form of frivolity on the ice today."

Reassured, he briskly undertook the organization of the trip after breakfast. Soon both carriages were filled, and the coachmen made their way carefully along the icy streets, down whose middle a lane had been cleared, leaving huge banks of snow on each side of the corridor.

She was surprised that Mr. Belvedere had come, and still more surprised to hear him tell the tale of Boudicca and her vengeance against the Romans in such hair-raising terms that Monty was looking fairly wild-eyed by the end of their ride.

Eventually they reached the river, and the passengers stepped out eagerly into the cold. The watermen who normally ran the taxis across the Thames had put up signs to inform the public that the ice was safe and that they could walk straight to the other side of the river without benefit of taxi, although some of the more enterprising ones had cut channels in the riverbank and offered to help the fairgoers across for twopence. By the time Elise and her group had reached the Thames, hundreds of people had availed themselves of that privilege, and they joined the others that had come to see the opening of the fair.

A sprinkling of booths had arisen, offering food and drink to sustain those walking across the Thames. The most popular one, at which they stopped toward the end of the afternoon, offered Lapland mutton, a rather fanciful name given to the sheep they were roasting. The group paused briefly, several of them sampling the mutton and a number of the gentlemen partaking of the grog offered in the neighboring booth.

"It appears that the fair is assembling itself, but is not quite together yet," observed James Gray as they walked past the scattered booths erected on the ice. "This is interesting, but I daresay that tomorrow there will be twice—or perhaps thrice—as many booths."

"Oh, we should definitely come back!" agreed Olivia, who was still nibbling at her slice of Lapland mutton. "And I did see a booth with ribbons and laces that I would like to stop at before we leave."

"Whatever you wish to do, Livy," Elise said indulgently, and the group made its way back to the ribbons. There Olivia purchased scarlet ribbons to her heart's content while the others poked about among the tents that were being erected.

"Gambling," said Monty briefly, returning from one of his forays and pointing to a large striped tent in the distance. "Setting it all up in a tent—roulette, hazard, whatever you please—to bring in the flats to spend their money."

"I shall go home and count my shillings," said Nigel. "Tomorrow could be my lucky day, and if Mama's Twelfth Night fortune is correct, I should not wish to miss it. I shall need every additional shilling possible."

Charles nodded. "Costly business, having children,"

he agreed. "No need to fill that cradle though, Nigel. I'd be happy to lend you one of mine. Two or three, even."

"That warms my heart almost as much as finding that charm in my cake," returned Nigel dryly.

"Want to watch yourself if you gamble out here," advised Monty briefly. "Captain Sharps, every last man jack of them!"

"Monty! You shock me!" exclaimed his brother. Seeing his brother's expression, Nigel patted his hand. "Never mind. I was only joking, Monty. I know perfectly well not to risk a penny in there or in any other of the little hells they erect for the occasion."

Relieved, Monty gave his attention to the rest of the flock. A fair could be serious business, and not only the sheep were fleeced there. While Nigel was awake upon almost every suit, Monty had had a little more experience among the charlatans. He did not claim to be a downy one, but he was not a flat, either. And he did not wish to have to explain to Ravinia how it was that Nigel had shed every penny that he owned at a gambling hell set upon the River Thames during a frost fair.

While Monty was tangling with serious problems, Elise had wandered off among the booths and peddlers, enjoying herself hugely. She had not experienced so much freedom since she had left Brookston Hall. She wandered at will, never minding whether she was accompanied by maid or chaperon. Suddenly she realized, however, that she did have an escort.

"Mr. Gray!" she said, smiling. "I did not know that you were close by."

He bowed and smiled in return. "How could I bring myself to be very far away, Miss MacGregor?" he inquired gently.

Elise looked into his tender eyes and responded, "How indeed, sir?"

For a moment, that exchange was enough, for the

warmth of his response buoyed her spirits. Suddenly, however, she was aware that she must learn the answer to Mr. Belvedere's question, and she wanted to do so delicately. By no means did she wish to embarrass either herself or him.

"Mr. Gray," Elise said slowly, measuring the words that she really did not wish to say, "may I ask you a question?"

He smiled more tenderly still. "But of course you may, Miss MacGregor," he answered.

"You have said so many lovely things to me," she responded, "about my hair and my complexion and my manner. You have given me beautiful compliments that any young woman would treasure."

"They have been easy to say because they are true," he said gently.

"You are too kind, sir," she said lightly, forcing herself to smile. "But you knew all the while you said them, Mr. Gray, that I was engaged to be wed, did you not?" To her own surprise, she managed to say it in such a way that it was no more than a teasing question, one to which she already knew the answer so that he felt no unease.

A short pause ensued, while he looked at her, gazed off into space, and then brought back his tender gaze to focus upon her. "I confess it," he sighed. "I knew that in the end my heart must be broken, yet I was drawn to you in spite of that."

Elise smiled. "Or perhaps because of that," she teased. "After all, it is far safer to flirt with a woman who has no expectations of you other than pretty words and pretty behavior."

He nodded, his eyes twinkling. "That is very true, of course. It is most difficult to have an elegant flirtation when one is in constant fear of being taken too seriously."

"I can see that that could present quite a problem for an eligible young gentleman, Mr. Gray, and take a great deal of joy from the flirtation."

He took her gloved hand and raised it to her lips. "We understand one another very well, ma'am," he assured her. "I must tell you that I have the highest regard for both your charm and your good sense."

She inclined her head demurely to acknowledge the tribute, happy at least that she had brought this episode to a graceful end with no embarrassment.

Mr. Gray continued to hold her hand, however, and his dark eyes had become suddenly serious. "I believe that I am going to be obliged to renounce my flirtations, however," he told her, no teasing in his voice now. "For I think that I have finally found a young woman to whom I shall wish to give all my time."

Startled by this unexpected shift of tone, Elise's heart began to thump. Was it possible that she had misunderstood him after all?

She summoned all her self-control. "What do you mean, Mr. Gray?" she asked calmly.

"Would you like to know her name?" he asked, still holding her hand and looking at her intently.

Elise nodded her head.

"Miss Olivia MacGregor," he said quietly. "I have never met anyone quite like your sister."

"Livy?" responded Elise blankly.

Mr. Gray nodded. "I know that she is young, so naturally I would not press my suit yet, nor would I trifle with her affections." He hesitated a moment, and when she did not respond, he said, "Since you were so honest with me, I thought that I could tell you, Miss MacGregor."

"Of course you may—as indeed you have," she responded crisply. "Naturally you have said nothing to Livy about this."

He looked wounded. "Naturally not—although she may suspect my feeling. It is difficult for me to hide. I have been completely captivated from the night at the theater when you had me sit next to her to protect her from young Townsend."

A sudden explosion of movement and noise announced the arrival of the Terrors in their vicinity. They looked up to see their group rounding the corner of Monty's gambling tent, the Terrors moving at a gallop. Mr. Belvedere had Livy's arm, but Monty had been called into action with Charles to restrain Reginald and Theodore, so Mr. Townsend, ever hopeful, was drawing near.

"Shall we join the others, Mr. Gray?" she murmured. "I believe that Mr. Townsend is closing in once again."

"Ah, yes!" he exclaimed, offering her his arm. "By all means we must rescue Miss Olivia."

Elise closed her eyes briefly as they walked toward the others. He was quite correct, of course, in everything he said. They had simply enjoyed a brief and pleasing flirtation, and she had made more of it than she should have. At least no one knew of her foolish attachment, she congratulated herself—except for Mr. Belvedere, of course—and he really did not matter. And as for Livy's feelings for Mr. Gray, she would have to discover the truth of the matter, for Livy had as yet given her no indication of any attachment on her part. She hoped there was none. Livy was too young.

By the time the carriages arrived back in Darlington Square that afternoon, Elise could scarcely wait to get out and return to her room. Her face was stiff from maintaining a pleasant expression during the last part of their time at the fair and the ride home. At least, she thought, a little rest would help her to come to terms with the situation.

She did not, however, have very much time alone. Soon after she had lain down, one of the maids came in with a salver. Not wishing to speak to anyone, Elise had kept her eyes closed, and the girl had made up the fire once more and then withdrawn quietly from the room. When Elise finally opened her eyes again, she could see the salver that the maid had brought in on a table by the fire. On it lay a letter.

Elise sat in front of the fire for several minutes before she had the courage to break the wafer and open it. At least it was from her father instead of Mr. Westbrook. Her stomach was painfully knotted, and her throat had constricted so tightly that she wasn't certain she could swallow.

Finally she forced herself to read it. Her father, always kind, remained so even now. If she did not wish to marry Robert Westbrook, her father wrote, then she need not do so. He thought it a regrettable decision, but no legal documents had been signed and, he added, even if they had been, Mr. Westbrook was an honorable, proud man and he would not, after due consideration, have insisted upon the marriage.

He had come to Brookston Hall, of course, but Mr. MacGregor had told him that the final decision to break the engagement or to go on with the marriage lay with her. When Mr. Westbrook had spoken of Elise's affections having become engaged elsewhere, her father had assumed that she had shared the same information with Mr. Westbrook that she had with him, and he had agreed that she appeared to be very attached to James Gray, a gentleman she had met in London, and that indeed she might be considering marriage.

Elise sat perfectly still, afraid of reading more. Finally, she forced herself to go on.

Now, her father continued, Mr. Westbrook wished to be satisfied that he had made his case for continuing their engagement as strongly as possible.

Elise finished reading the letter, folded it up carefully, then opened it again and reread it to be certain that she understood its contents. Then she folded it up once more, placed it on her lap, and sat staring into the fire.

Mr. Westbrook still wished to marry her.

Mr. Westbrook believed her to be engaged, or very nearly so, to James Gray.

And Mr. Westbrook was on his way to London.

For a moment she stared at the tiny wishbone, shining in the firelight. Even if it possessed magical powers, she thought sadly, one wish would not help her now. She would not give way and marry him, however, for she had truly realized how uncomfortable she would be with him—a stern, unsmiling man. She knew that she required humor and kindness in the man she married.

Seventeen

When Elise arose the next morning, she felt as heavy as lead. Olivia watched her with concern and insisted upon checking her brow for fever.

"Perhaps we shouldn't go to the fair today," she said, "for you do look quite dreadful, Elise."

For a moment Elise felt a flicker of hope. Livy was right; she didn't feel well, and she could stay home. Then she wouldn't have to face other people for a little while. Of course, no one else knew of her problem at the moment, but they would soon enough. Mr. Westbrook could arrive at any time now. If the letter from her father could make it to London, she knew that the chances were excellent that Mr. Westbrook would soon make it as well, despite the dreadful weather.

Elise straightened her shoulders and forced herself to smile at her sister. "I shall feel much better once I have had breakfast," she said. "But before we go down, Livy, I should like to ask you something."

"What is it?" asked Olivia, still watching her with a worried expression. "Did you have bad news from Papa? Aunt said that you had received a letter, but you were asleep when I came in last night, so I didn't wish to trouble you."

"No, all is well there, Livy. My question is about someone here."

"Someone here? What do you mean? Was Papa asking

about Arthur Townsend? He is a bother, of course, but not anything for Papa to worry about."

Elise shook her head. "No, I wasn't thinking of Mr. Townsend." She paused a moment. "Is there anyone, Livy, who has captured your interest since we have been in London?"

Olivia colored prettily and looked down at her hands before replying. "Do you mean a gentleman?"

"Yes," replied Elise.

Elise waited patiently and finally her sister met her eyes and nodded. "I wanted to say something about it to you, Elise, but it—somehow it didn't seem fair to you to do so."

"Fair to me?" asked Elise, startled. She had thought that she had kept her feelings about James Gray reasonably well hidden. "What do you mean?"

"You know what your position is," said Olivia, reaching out to take Elise's hand and hold it tightly, "engaged to a man that you don't give a farthing for. I could see the difference in your spirits as soon as we arrived here and we met Mr. Gray. How could I tell you that I had discovered someone that I find—very interesting—when you are still bound to Mr. Westbrook? It seemed too selfish to mention."

"Nonsense!" said Elise briskly. "I am made of sturdier stuff than that, Livy! How could your being happy be a selfish thing?"

"Then you don't mind?" asked Olivia, her eyes brightening. "It had sometimes seemed to me as though you felt a certain interest in—"

"Not at all!" said Elise hastily. "I have merely been amusing myself." She stood up and pulled Olivia to her feet. "Go down and have your breakfast, Livy, so that we will be ready to go to the fair!"

"What about you? Aren't you coming, too?"

"I'll be there in just a moment. I've got something to take care of first."

Satisfied that all was well, Olivia snatched up her shawl and hurried down to the dining room. As soon as she was out of sight, Elise made her way to Ravinia in the morning room. She did not really wish to do so, but she had decided that she must have help to solve her problem. Quietly she slipped in and laid the matter before her aunt.

"And so Livy fancies herself attached to young Gray, does she?" asked Ravinia, studying her niece carefully.

Elise nodded. "Although nothing has passed between them, Aunt, so you may rest easy there. And I have told her that I was merely amusing myself with a flirtation. She does not know that I ever felt anything more than that."

"But you did," said Ravinia, "since you wrote to my brother and Mr. Westbrook and called off the wedding."

Elise nodded silently.

"And so at any point Mr. Westbrook could show up here and he would find that the man for whom you have broken your engagement to him is now paying court to your sister."

Again Elise nodded. "And I don't know how to avoid having that happen. I've no wish to hurt Olivia, Aunt, and she would be unhappy if she knew that I felt any real affection for Mr. Gray. I also have absolutely no desire to become an object of pity, both here in your house and at home. Ours is a very small society, and the story would be known everywhere."

Ravinia nodded. "It would eventually become old hat, but you are quite right. Such a thing would be forgotten quickly in London, with so many other stories to take its place, but in a country society, it would linger for longer that you would like. At any rate, we must find a way to solve the problem."

For the first time since she had received the letter, Elise began to feel vaguely hopeful. If Ravinia Longfellow thought that a problem could be solved, Elise had no doubt that she could do it. She sat and watched as her aunt thoughtfully tapped the corner of her writing desk, considering possibilities. Suddenly her face lighted.

"You need what Diana Fotheringale called a Frost Fair fiancé!" she exclaimed triumphantly.

"Whatever is that?" asked Elise, bewildered.

"At the time of the last Frost Fair, Diana was a widow—between her second and her third husbands, I believe—and when she went to the fair with a young Frenchman, she was severely criticized for not being properly chaperoned. She announced that they were engaged, although they weren't, and that put a halt to the gossip."

Elise stared at her blankly.

"Well, don't you see?" demanded Ravinia. "It was just a temporary engagement to stop the gossip, and both of them knew it. Once the frost melted and the fair was over, so was the engagement! It was simply a diversionary technique."

"But, Aunt, I have no Frenchman handy," Elise pointed out reasonably.

"Walter!" said her aunt, after a few more minutes had passed in silence.

"I beg your pardon?" said Elise.

"Walter Belvedere! I don't know why I didn't think of him immediately! This will work to perfection!"

"You want Walter Belvedere to be my Frost Fair fiancé?" Elise demanded in disbelief. "He won't do it!" She did not add that she did not wish for him to do it.

"There you are mistaken, my dear," replied her aunt with satisfaction. "I know that he will do it. He won't be best pleased about it, I grant you, but he will unquestionably do it!"

"Why?" asked Elise bluntly.

"For the sake of seeing your father's collection of Roman bits and pieces that he has found at Brookston Hall," said Ravinia. "You saw his reaction to my father-in-law's notebook. I cannot imagine why I did not think of this earlier. I have been looking for ways to continue civilizing Walter Belvedere, and an engagement should be very helpful."

"And if I don't wish to be part of the civilizing process?" asked Elise, trying to picture herself engaged, even in fancy, to Mr. Belvedere.

"Would you prefer to have it known that you broke your engagement to Mr. Westbrook for the sake of James Gray?" asked her aunt.

"But I didn't really cry off just because of that!" Elise protested.

"You said yourself that people will take it that way, and you know that they will—unless you distract them."

"Oh, very well," said Elise, defeated. Mr. Belvedere appeared to be the lesser of the two evils—but not by much.

"I shall send for him immediately," said Ravinia, taking out paper and ink. "He will go to the fair with you today. You run along now and have your breakfast. And remember, Elise," she added as her niece started toward the door, "you are to watch your sister. A little flirtation is all very well, but I don't wish her left alone with Mr. Gray. I will tell Monty and Nigel that as well."

"I daresay that won't be a problem," said Elise. "I should be surprised if Arthur Townsend lets them out of his sight."

"You see," said her aunt in satisfaction, "even Mr. Townsend serves a purpose."

The family had assembled in the drawing room, part of them prepared for the fair, the rest prepared to see them off. Ravinia was the only one missing, and the others were growing impatient. When the drawing room door opened, they all looked up expectantly, but it was Beavers, and he had come to fetch Elise to the morning room.

Elise went, expecting the worst, and the worst occurred. Walter Belvedere was there, looking as grim as she felt, but Ravinia was smiling broadly.

"It will only be for a few days, Mr. Belvedere," she reminded him complacently, "and just think of the treat that lies in store for you at the end of that time."

Here she turned to Elise. "And you cannot look so glum, either. I am going to escort the pair of you into the drawing room and announce your engagement, and you both need to look suitably happy."

Both of them flinched, but she continued, undeterred. "I shall tell them that you have broken off your engagement to Mr. Westbrook, Elise, in favor of this new relationship. Since I am standing in place of your father, I have given you my blessing. Now, look happy, the pair of you!"

They might as well have been marching to the gallows, thought Elise as they walked down the passage to the drawing room. She smiled dutifully and Mr. Belvedere at least managed to look less fierce as Ravinia shared the great news with the family.

There was a moment of stunned silence, then Nigel said, "My congratulations to both of you—but, Belvedere, while I agree that Elise is a prize, are you certain that you have considered the family you are marrying into?"

Laughter followed his remark, easing some of the tension, and Charles added, "Yes, as I recall, you were fearful that our eccentricities would damage your reputation."

"Well, it seems most irregular to me," said Lucy stiffly. "I cannot imagine why you would jilt one—"

"What Lucy means is that she wishes you very happy," inserted Sally, coming over to hug Elise, "as do Edward and I."

Monty was the most enthusiastic of the group, kissing Elise and clapping Belvedere on the back until Nigel reminded him that the fair would be over with before they reached the outskirts of it. The same group that had attended the day before trooped out to the carriages, again leaving behind the younger ones. The only reason that Nigel was attending the fair at all was that his home was overrun by children and that he planned to spend all of his time snugly ensconced in tents warmed by braziers.

"In fact," said Nigel, as their carriage carried them to the Thames, "I propose that we find a large table in a good coffeehouse—with many braziers—and stay there for the day."

"But, Nigel," said Elise, "how will we see the rest of the fair?"

"We can see all that we need to as we walk to the coffeehouse when we arrive and from it when we depart," replied her cousin firmly. "We will spend the day there celebrating your engagement."

Here he glanced at Belvedere, who had been staring out the window. "Very sly, you two have been. I had no notion that such a thing was about to happen, and I pride myself upon being very observant."

"Well, we did need to be discreet," replied Elise. "After all, I had not made known the breaking of my engagement."

"Except to Mr. Belvedere," returned Nigel promptly.

"Of course. Except to Mr. Belvedere."

It was a great relief to reach the fair and to remove herself from Nigel's scrutiny. He was altogether too astute for her comfort. Mr. Belvedere had not appeared perturbed, but then she did not think that he had heard a word that had been said.

"My, look how much it has changed from yesterday!" exclaimed Sally as they looked out across the river.

The grand mall, a wide ice avenue lined with booths on either side, now extended from Blackfriars Bridge to London Bridge. The Terrors pulled them up short almost at once at a printing press that displayed pictures of the Frost Fair and poems about it. Each demanded one to take home, along with hot sausages from the next booth.

"It's going to be a very long and very expensive day, I fear," sighed Charles. "We have been here less than five minutes, and each of them has already spent at least fivepence."

"Do you see anything that looks like a coffeehouse?" demanded Nigel. "I knew that there were advantages to being tall."

The taller ones looked about them at the sea of tents, but Monty shook his head. "Have to keep walking, Nigel. Find one as we go."

Nigel moaned and turned the fur collar of his greatcoat up about his ears. The Terrors had already disappeared, this time into a tent that advertised a puppet show, the story of Aladdin, within.

"Well, at least that'll keep them busy for a few minutes," sighed their father, having paid for their tickets and purchased cups of chocolate to wash down the sausages.

"Look!" exclaimed Olivia. "Swings! Let's go!"

"In this cold?" demanded Nigel, horrified. "Livy, you're not going to swing, are you?"

"Of course I am! This cloak is wonderful and the muff is keeping my hands warm. I must go on the swings!"

Giving way to the inevitable, they watched Livy swing, a sturdy young man pushing her faithfully. However, by the time she dismounted, their number had decreased. Charles had seen a stall with books and had headed that way, hoping to find a newspaper. Nigel had spotted what appeared to be a coffeehouse and had rushed toward it, promising to hold seats for everyone. Edward and Sally had wandered off hand in hand, saying that they would be back in a little while. Mr. Gray and Mr. Townsend waited for Olivia faithfully, as did Monty.

Elise and Mr. Belvedere stood to one side, watching the scene.

"You might try to look a little happier," she told him. "I have seen men pitched from their mounts who looked happier than you do."

"I shall try to do better," he said. "Perhaps if I think about your father's collection, I will look more pleasant."

They watched Olivia being helped from the swing and escorted to the gate where the others were waiting.

"Just when did you break your engagement, Miss MacGregor?" he asked abruptly. "And why?"

"I cannot see why that should matter to you, sir. It has nothing to do with our—arrangement." She could not bring herself to say engagement.

"Mr. Gray knew about your engagement, didn't he?" was the next question.

Outraged by his questions, Elise glared at him. "Naturally he did," she replied coldly. "He is a friend of my cousins."

"And so he felt perfectly free to flirt with you, did he not?" continued Belvedere relentlessly.

"Naturally that would be the only reason he would have to flirt with me!" she agreed bitterly, and turned away.

"Did I say that?" demanded Belvedere. "It was simply a convenient protection for him. I wonder how he will protect himself from Miss Olivia—or, more precisely, how she will protect herself from him!"

"You take a great interest in my sister's welfare, sir!" she observed sharply. "May I ask why?"

"Because she is a very pleasant young woman and a very vulnerable one!" he retorted. "She needs to be protected!"

"And I do not?"

"No more so than scorpions or tigers or other deadly creatures!" he replied, turning away.

"By all means, go and protect her then!" she exclaimed, anger flooding through her as she walked off into the crowd. She had no desire to see him waiting in line to protect Livy. She could not think how she was going to be able to survive this Frost Fair engagement. In fact, she was beginning to think that facing Mr. Westbrook and admitting the truth—that she had fallen temporarily in love with a man who cared not a fig for her—would be preferable to maintaining this mockery with Walter Belvedere.

Suddenly aware that she was freezing, Elise marched into the next tent she saw, hoping that it was warm. The interior was warmed with braziers and lighted with lanterns, and she could smell the simmering fragrance of hot cider. Seeing a keg that was apparently supposed to serve as a chair, she made herself comfortable. Taking a page from Nigel's book, she placed the keg as close to a brazier as she dared. A young man was singing, his voice soft and clear, and Elise gave herself over to the warmth and the darkness and the music, trying to forget her anger for the moment.

"A lovers' quarrel, Miss MacGregor?" inquired a familiar voice.

"Mr. Gray! What are you doing here?" she asked, opening her eyes.

"I am buying you a cup of hot cider, ma'am," he said, placing one in her hand.

She accepted it with gratitude, but she was watching him curiously. "But why aren't you with Livy?" she asked.

"You told me yesterday how you feel about her. Why give up the opportunity to be near her?"

He sighed and sat down next to her. "Because I cannot be near her," he said. "Everyone else is there. When I realized that you had disappeared, it was because your fiancé had pressed Arthur Townsend out of the way—as well as me and Monty. I could see no reason to stay and watch him with her. And I wondered where you had gotten off to, and why Belvedere had let you go."

She shrugged. "I suppose he finds my sister as charming as you do," she replied, trying to keep her voice light.

"He is a foolish man, to walk away from you," observed Gray, looking at her in the familiar way that made her melt inside.

Why could he look at her as though he cared deeply when she knew it wasn't the case at all? And why did she still respond when she knew he was only flirting?

Elise had no satisfactory answers for herself. "You should go back to the others, Mr. Gray—to Olivia."

"And so should you, ma'am—to Mr. Belvedere. Shall we go back together?"

She shook her head. "I'm not going. I'm staying right here until it is time for us to return. When I think it is late enough, I will try to find all of you out close to the printing press where we came in."

"Very well," he responded, and took another sip of his cider.

"Aren't you leaving, Mr. Gray?"

"No. I plan to stay with you, Miss MacGregor, both because you should not be alone in the crowd and because I wish to be with you."

He smiled and tucked a stray curl back into the hood of her cloak. "Because I believe I underestimated the power of your charm, ma'am. We ended our flirtation only yesterday, and yet already I miss you."

Elise took another sip of the hot cider and allowed

herself to relax a little bit. He was only flirting, of course, but it was a delightful exchange, and she slipped back into it with ease.

And so the afternoon passed quickly by without their even noticing. James Gray ordered food, and they ate and drank more cider and listened to the young man sing as they flirted with one another most happily.

"It's good to see that the two of you are snug and warm!" snapped Walter Belvedere, appearing beside them suddenly.

"Yes, we are. Thank you, Mr. Belvedere, for being concerned about us," responded Elise, looking up at his angry face with an untroubled smile.

"And I don't suppose it troubles you to know that the rest of us are cold and tired, or to know that we have been searching for you for hours? Your sister is distraught!"

"Well, there we have the heart of the matter," replied Elise. "You are concerned because my sister has been upset."

"Try for once to be reasonable, Miss MacGregor, and to let your mind rule your actions instead of your emotions! The two of you need to come back with me now so that we can go to the carriages and the others can go home and get warm. Try to show a little common civility!"

"I would hate to cause the others any discomfort, Mr. Gray," said Elise, ignoring Belvedere. "Perhaps we should go back now."

"If you think so, Miss MacGregor, we shall by all means go," he replied, standing and offering her his arm. Together they walked out, leaving Belvedere to trail after them.

"Problems in paradise, I believe," murmured Nigel, seeing them return. "I do hope that we can get home without a row."

Nigel's wish was granted, largely because no one spoke

on the way back. Everyone in their carriage was either exhausted, frozen, angry, or confused.

As they got ready for bed that evening, Elise decided that she must make an effort with her sister, so she said, "And did you enjoy Mr. Gray's company today, Livy?"

Olivia shrugged. "He was very nice."

"That's faint praise indeed, Livy—particularly compared with what you said about him this morning."

"This morning?" asked Livy, puzzled.

"When you were telling me about the gentleman you found so interesting. Don't you recall our discussion before coming down to breakfast today?"

Olivia looked at her for a moment without speaking, but finally she turned her face away and said, "It was not Mr. Gray I was speaking of. It was Mr. Belvedere."

Eighteen

Elise plucked at the covers that night long after Olivia had sunk into a peaceful sleep. Naturally she had imagined that Livy was speaking of Mr. Gray rather than Mr. Belvedere because James Gray was so much more attractive a man—much more charming and self-possessed, precisely the kind of gentleman a young girl would find appealing. That, of course, was because she herself had found him so.

But Walter Belvedere? He had been very kind to Livy, of course, and undoubtedly that accounted for part of the attraction. And, Elise had to admit to herself, he did indeed seem a much different man than he had when she first met him and he had so insulted her and Mr. Gray at his parents' ball. Still, he was direct, rather than subtle, and he had no patience with matters he considered trivial or behavior he considered misleading. Too, it would be better if he were a little less certain that he was always correct. How could Livy find him so appealing?

As she thought through that morning's conversation with Olivia that she had misunderstood so badly, Elise suddenly remembered that her sister had started to say that she had thought Elise had shown a certain interest in the gentleman, but Elise had cut her off hurriedly, thinking that she meant to go on and say that Elise felt a *tendre* for Mr. Gray. But certainly Livy could have seen nothing that would make her think that she felt an interest in Mr. Belvedere!

What a mess it all was, she thought unhappily. And in a few short hours she would be expected to go happily out to the fair with her fiancé and act as though her world were all in order. Of course, everyone knew that she and Belvedere had had a disagreement today, but she could not afford to let it continue indefinitely. Or could she? She lay there a moment, the glimmer of an idea taking shape. Finally she smiled and relaxed, able now to sleep at last.

Very early the next morning she once again went to see her aunt, and found Ravinia waiting to hear her report. Her eyebrows lifted as she listened to her niece's somewhat abridged account of yesterday's activities. Instead of speaking of the quarrel, Elise concentrated most of her time on the confusion that had arisen with Olivia and their conversation about the gentleman she was interested in.

"And so you misunderstood Olivia? It is really Walter Belvedere for whom she feels an attachment, rather than Mr. Gray?" demanded Ravinia. "How came you to make such a mistake?"

"It was natural enough, Aunt!" protested Elise. "Livy gave no name, and of course I assumed that—"

"You assumed that, since you do not find Belvedere attractive, no one else would either?" her aunt finished crisply.

Hearing it stated as baldly as that was embarrassing, but it was the truth. Elise nodded.

"Well, now you see that that is not the case." Ravinia smiled, thinking it over. "Actually, a little flirtation would do them both good—if he were not betrothed to you, naturally. At least Livy would not come to any harm at the hands of Walter Belvedere."

"Neither would she with Mr. Gray!" retorted Elise defensively.

"I am far less certain of that," remarked Ravinia, "although if he cares for her as you say he does, then you might be correct. Otherwise, she could simply expect to have her heart broken."

She looked at Elise for a moment. "When this is all over, a lasting connection between your sister and Belvedere—after Olivia has her Season, of course— might be just the thing."

"Are you saying that Livy might *marry* Mr. Belvedere!" exclaimed Elise in horror. "Aunt, you cannot mean it!"

Ravinia shrugged. "I do not see why not. If they care for one another, he is of good family and he is basically a good man, if somewhat eccentric. He would treat Olivia well."

Elise shook her head. "It would never do!" she said. "It would not work!"

"Why do you think that it would not?" asked her aunt, interested. "I can see no obstacles. He even has a deep interest that your father shares. They would probably end by living at Brookston Hall, and your father would be delighted."

Elise was at a loss for words. It was unthinkable. For a moment she tried to picture herself at the breakfast table at Brookston Hall with her father and Livy, with Walter Belvedere at her sister's side, but she could not bring herself to do it. She would have to call him "brother" and see him regularly—every day, if she were still living at home.

She shook her head again. "It would not work," she repeated.

"Well, that of course is neither here nor there," agreed her aunt comfortably. "What we must concern ourselves with is today. You told me that you had an idea."

"It sounds very peculiar," said Elise hesitantly, "but

then having a Frost Fair fiancé sounds most peculiar, too."

"What is it that you wish to do?"

"Yesterday, Mr. Belvedere and I had a disagreement—"

"Yes, I know," said Ravinia. "I heard that you ran away from the others and that you and Mr. Gray spent the majority of the day together."

Elise blushed. "I thought that perhaps Livy and I could switch partners, so to speak—for today at least."

Ravinia stared at her. "You are engaged, and you wish to switch partners?" she said.

"We are not truly engaged, Aunt! You know that!" Elise exclaimed.

"Yes, but you and Mr. Belvedere are the only ones aware of that," her aunt pointed out reasonably. She looked at Elise's downcast expression and relented a little. "Well, you certainly cannot announce that you are switching Mr. Belvedere for Mr. Gray, but it would do no harm for the four of you to be together, and then you could see how things develop."

Feeling happier than she had for what seemed like days, Elise bent over and kissed her aunt on the cheek.

"Actually, it will probably work quite well," called her aunt after her. "I daresay Belvedere will be pleased to be with Olivia."

Elise closed the door to the morning room a little more sharply than was necessary, but her mood was restored almost immediately. She was going to the fair in the company of James Gray! Livy had no interest in him, so she would not be hurting her sister. Walter Belvedere would be there, of course, but that was merely an inconvenience. When she went in to breakfast, the spring was back in her step and the light in her eye.

"Well, Elise," drawled Nigel, "I had feared that you would emerge red-eyed and depressed after your lovers' spat yesterday. Yet here you are, looking full of vim and

vigor. Although being engaged to Belvedere appears to
have its hills and valleys, you seem to be taking it well."

Not even his mention of Belvedere and the engagement could overset her this morning. "It makes life
more interesting, Nigel," she said cheerfully, stacking
her plate with toast and plum cake.

"Feeling well, are you, Elise?" inquired Monty uneasily.
He had not understood the events of yesterday well at
all. An engaged couple, so far as he knew, behaved like
an engaged couple. He had seen Elise kissing Mr. Belvedere, but he had seen no lover-like behavior between
them yesterday—except the quarreling, of course. He relaxed slightly as he thought of it that way. Of course
there would be trouble. He saw it all the time among his
married friends. In fact, that had contributed heavily to
his own desire to remain a bachelor.

Elise nodded. "I am ready for the adventures of the
day, Monty," she assured him. "Livy and I have donned
our warmest garments and Livy is wearing the scarlet ribbons that she bought at the fair. What do you suppose we
shall do there today?"

"Live in the coffeehouse beside the brazier," said Nigel
promptly. "It was really much more bearable than I had
expected. The only time I was truly cold was when Monty
and Livy wrenched me from my cozy corner to come in
search of you, cousin."

"At least you got to see a little of the fair because of
that, Nigel," she observed unrepentantly.

"I did not," he assured her. "My breath immediately
frosted my eyelashes so heavily that it was difficult to see.
I was very nearly blinded."

"Very nearly put you on one of those donkeys," said
Monty. A number of the nimble-footed creatures were for
hire, trotting up and down on the City Road down the
center of the fair. "Needed to look where you were going.
Tripped three times, the last time into a lady's lap."

"I was never certain whether she was pretty or not," complained Nigel. "I couldn't see clearly enough."

"Husband wasn't pretty," Monty informed him. "Thought you was three parts disguised and wanted to plant you a facer."

"Why didn't he?" asked Elise, interested. "Plant Nigel a facer, that is?"

Monty grinned. "Fobbed him off with a Banbury tale. Told him Nigel's sweetheart had walked away with a soldier and he'd half frozen trying to find her."

The others laughed and Charles commented, "You are constantly surprising me with your resourcefulness, Monty. That is why today I shall leave you in charge of Reginald and Theodore."

Monty suddenly looked as though his breakfast had revolted against him. "Beg pardon?" he said weakly.

Charles nodded expansively. "I'm going to the club today," he announced. "The boys will be fine with you, Monty. I have a world of confidence in you. You may take my carriage."

Before Monty could gather his wits and protest, his brother had left the room briskly and was undoubtedly on his way out the door, grabbing his greatcoat and cane from Beavers.

"Doomed," said Monty, staring at his coffee bleakly.

"They will be fine," said Elise encouragingly. "After all, Edward and Sally will be there, too."

Monty brightened at this, and appeared able to swallow his coffee once more. His confidence was misplaced, however, for Edward put in an appearance just moments later, announcing that the twins had caught Marjorie's cold and so he and Sally would be staying at home.

When the two carriages pulled away that morning, Monty, Mr. Townsend, Nigel, and the Terrors occupied one; Elise, Olivia, Mr. Gray, and Mr. Belvedere, the other. Nigel had done his best to get into the other carriage, but Monty had proved implacable. Nigel rode with him.

Once at the fair, Reginald and Theodore made their way directly to a skittles game, tracked briskly by Monty, who also had a firm grip on his brother's arm. Nigel looked longingly at the coffeehouse where he had spent yesterday, but his brother escorted him briskly by it. The others, including Mr. Townsend, went strolling among the maze of tents, trying to decide what to do first.

Suddenly Olivia stopped and put her hand to her throat.

"What's wrong, Livy?" asked her sister.

"I must have left my scarf in the coach," she replied. "I wanted it to wrap around the lower part of my face so that I could breathe more easily."

"Please allow me to fetch it, Miss Olivia," offered Mr. Townsend promptly. "I should like to be of service."

"Why thank you, Mr. Townsend," she replied sweetly. "You are very kind."

Highly gratified, Arthur Townsend turned and hurried back in the direction of the coach.

"I don't recall seeing a scarf," murmured Elise thoughtfully.

"With very good reason," replied her sister in a low voice, smiling complacently.

Together, the two couples made their way to a sleigh, which was offering rides the length of the fair. Mr. Belvedere handed in Elise, and Mr. Gray assisted Olivia, but somehow by the time they were all seated, Mr. Belvedere sat beside Olivia, and Mr. Gray beside Elise. The two couples faced one another, and after the lap robes were tucked around them, they moved smoothly across the ice, watching the panoply of the fair unfold. Bright streamers and flags floated in the icy breeze above a sea of tents and booths. Almost overnight a whole new world had sprung into being, and London was on holiday.

They passed a merry-go-round, its riders spinning happily in the winter sunshine.

"Do you suppose the Terrors will take Monty and Nigel there?" asked Olivia.

Mr. Belvedere shook his head. "Too tame," he remarked. "They will be looking for something livelier. If they could increase the speed so that the riders might be tossed off, they would consider riding it."

"Longfellow shouldn't take the care of those boys so seriously," said Mr. Gray with pity. "He makes too much of the problem. After all, they're only boys. What mischief can they get into?"

The other three exchanged significant glances, but did not pursue the matter. If Monty's luck was in today, Mr. Gray was correct. Reginald and Theodore would get into no trouble at all.

"Now this is my idea of a perfect day," sighed Olivia, looking out at the lively scene with contentment, "to spend the day doing nothing but seeking pleasure in the company of friends."

James Gray smiled at her. "A delightful observation, Miss Olivia," he said. "I quite agree with you. I can think of nothing better."

A pause ensued and then Olivia said tentatively, "And what of you, Mr. Belvedere? Is this not your notion of a perfect day?"

To Elise's annoyance, he also smiled down pleasantly at Livy. She knew very well that a pleasant smile did not come to him readily, and it irritated her too that he had obviously been attending to what Livy had said. Had she been the one speaking, she was certain that he would not have heard a word.

"Aside from the fact that it is a pleasure to be with you—with all of you," he added, glancing up belatedly at Elise and Mr. Gray, "I would have to say that my notion of a perfect day is quite different."

"But how?" Livy asked anxiously. "What would you wish to be doing?"

"Looking into the past," he replied, "just as I was doing with Mrs. Longfellow's notebook. I find it fascinating, and it is that work which makes it pleasant for me to get up each morning and begin the day."

James Gray gently elbowed Elise, and gave her a significant glance as she looked sidewise at him. Clearly, he thought Walter Belvedere extremely strange. Elise was certain that, for the moment at least, he had forgotten that she was supposed to be engaged to the man.

"I must say that sounds quite dreary to me," said Gray. "I still agree with Miss Olivia."

A brief silence fell once more, and then it apparently occurred to Mr. Gray that no one had asked Elise for her opinion. She had noticed it, naturally, but she was not surprised. They were both too absorbed in Olivia. Or at least Mr. Gray was, and whatever attention Mr. Belvedere could spare from history was given to Olivia.

"And, Miss MacGregor, what of you?" said Mr. Gray. "Do you side with your sister and me, or, like Mr. Belvedere, do you favor the past? What is your notion of the perfect day?"

"I believe that I can answer that," said Walter Belvedere, and the other three stared at him in surprise. "I should imagine that Miss MacGregor would enjoy spending her time in the shops, looking for pretty things to adorn herself so that she could join hosts of other attractive people looking at one another in the evening, all of them trying to decide who was most—luminous."

"What absolute rubbish!" snapped Elise, the sudden color in her cheeks having nothing to do with the cold. "How dare you assume that you know me well enough to say such a thing, sir? And you are, of course, aside from being insufferably arrogant and condescending, completely incorrect!"

Another silence fell over the sleigh, and even the driver cocked an eye back over his shoulder to survey the scene. Olivia stared at her sister as though she had never seen her before. Elise never became angry, and she certainly never insulted anyone. Mr. Gray, accustomed to more polished conversation, looked decidedly uneasy. Only Mr. Belvedere appeared entirely comfortable. He merely looked calmly at Elise, the trace of a smile on his lips. Elise noticed it immediately.

"And you needn't look at me in such an odiously smug way!" she added. "It must grow tiresome, looking down at the rest of us from your superior height of intelligence!"

"Not really," he replied, his tone reflective. "To be honest, I very seldom look in that direction."

For a moment Elise longed for some of the Terrors' rocks. She had the perfect target for them, and her muff would not make a satisfactory substitute.

The rest of the ride passed in a strained silence. Olivia and Mr. Gray did not wish to speak for fear of setting Elise off once more. Elise was too angry to speak, and Mr. Belvedere appeared to be thinking of other things.

As soon as they descended from the sleigh, Olivia and Mr. Gray looked at each other desperately.

"What about a cup of tea or chocolate?" suggested Mr. Gray, seeing the sign on a nearby tent. "We might as well have some refreshment and warm ourselves just a little."

"Perhaps we'll see Nigel," said Olivia, attempting to lighten the atmosphere.

The other two followed them silently in, and Olivia guided her sister to a table while the gentlemen went to purchase their drinks.

"Elise," she whispered, "whatever is wrong? I have never seen you so angry before."

Elise had had time to swallow her anger and to regret her sudden loss of composure. She smiled and at-

tempted to put the best face on things that she could
manage.

"It's nothing, Livy," she said soothingly. "It's just that
Mr. Belvedere and I—that we had a misunderstanding."

Olivia nodded. "That happened yesterday. That's why
you went away by yourself." She looked at her sister seriously. "But I thought that was all taken care of. You
didn't appear to be quarreling until just now, and I
didn't see what he had done that made you so terriby
upset."

Elise patted her sister's hand. "It's really not anything
that you need worry about, Livy. I promise you that you
need not concern yourself about it."

Olivia looked unconvinced, but a lifetime with Elise
had taught her that her sister was normally very much in
control of every situation, so she accepted her assurance.
After a moment, she said, "Elise, do you think that Mr.
Belvedere really meant what he said when he described
his perfect day?"

Elise looked at her in surprise. "Yes, I am certain that
he did. You saw him at our aunt's home, Livy. He sat up
all night, reading and making notes. He does not be-
grudge any amount of time spent on his studies."

Livy sighed. "I suppose you are right. But when he
skated with me at the Serpentine, he talked of other
things, too, and I supposed—well, I thought that he was
just like other gentlemen, only that he liked to read
about history now and then."

"I think it is considerably more than that. You remember how surprised you were that he took the time
to come and skate, so you do know how he spends his
days when he has a choice in the matter."

"Yes," said Olivia, brightening, "and he was so very
kind to come and help me. And he was so pleasant about
it, too, not as though he had been dragged there under
protest."

"Yes, I know," agreed Elise, thinking with annoyance of how unusual that was for Mr. Belvedere.

"Elise, I'm very glad that you are not marrying Mr. Westbrook, for you know what I thought of that, but—"

"But what, Livy?" Elise asked when she did not continue.

"Forgive me for saying this, Elise, but you need not become engaged to someone else simply so that you do not have to marry Mr. Westbrook. You know that you can simply cry off."

Olivia had struck entirely too close to the truth, and Elise winced a little. Still, she forced herself to smile. "I will not do anything that makes me unhappy, Livy. I promise you that."

Here the gentlemen returned, and the conversation became general and, to the relief of Olivia and Mr. Gray, pleasant. Elise was determined not to allow Mr. Belvedere to throw her off balance again, and Mr. Belvedere said nothing inflammatory.

The afternoon slipped by pleasantly enough. Elise and Olivia rode sidesaddle on two of the ponies that were resolutely giving rides to children and slender young ladies. As they were waiting their turn, they saw the owner turn away a very large, solid-looking woman. He had stared at the woman in disbelief when she took out twopence for her ride, and asked if she planned to kill the poor animal on the spot.

"I wouldn't eat that gingerbread, Miss MacGregor," said Mr. Belvedere in a low voice. They had just purchased squares of hot gingerbread before getting into line for the ponies. "I should hate for you to be turned away as she was."

Elise started to reply angrily at this unwarranted insult to her size, but she glanced up in time to see his lips quivering, and finished her gingerbread with aplomb, ignoring his sally.

Thinking of the children that had been left at home,

they paused at a booth filled with toys, all of them labeled "bought on the river Thames."

"For which you undoubtedly pay three times the normal price," commented Mr. Belvedere dryly, holding up a top and examining it doubtfully.

"Certainly," replied Elise. "The shopkeepers have trundled these out from their proper homes to the ice and paid the price of setting up a tent and extra tables to display their goods. Naturally they must make their expenses and a profit."

He grinned at her. "I am relieved to hear that the shopkeepers have a champion," he replied. She waited for him to add that he would have expected as much, since she undoubtedly spent more than half of her life in the shops, but he did not.

Almost disappointed, she returned to inspecting the wares. Suddenly, however, someone seized her by the arm.

"Seen the Terrors?" Monty gasped, leaning against her. Nigel, looking equally out of breath, stood behind him.

Elise shook her head. "Have they been gone long?"

"Long enough to do damage somewhere," said Nigel. "I've never had such a day in all my life—nor do I intend ever to have one like it again. Charles may keep his children himself!"

"Got to find them!" said Monty, looking wild-eyed. "Headed in this direction, but they could have doubled back."

"We'll take the sleigh," said Belvedere. "We will go more quickly and we can see more from it."

One was passing in the distance, and they watched as he ran out and stopped it, explained the situation to the driver and passengers, paid them double the price of their ride for getting out early, and then signaled to the others to come. They packed themselves into the sleigh. Monty and Nigel, still panting, collapsed in relief.

"I thought my lungs would burst," Nigel said. "Monty wouldn't allow me to slow down at all."

"No telling where they've gotten to or what they've done!" said Monty grimly, trying to look in all directions at once.

As they approached London Bridge, he stood up and pointed. "There!" he cried.

At the very outskirts of the fair, they could see two small figures, dark against the snow. They were headed toward upheavals of ice that looked like small mountains in the distance.

"Faster, man!" said Belvedere to the driver, pointing to the boys, but the driver shook his head.

"Don't go beyond the fair booths," he said. "Can't risk my rig on the ice there."

"Do you mean it's not safe out there?" demanded Elise, also standing to look.

The driver shook his head. "Wouldn't give a farthing for their chances beyond that ridge."

Olivia had also stood up and was calling the boys' names as loudly as she could.

"Don't waste your breath," advised Monty. "Can't hear you or won't stop!" As the driver came to a halt, he leaped from the sleigh and started running. The ice was rough here, but it was still difficult going. Mr. Belvedere and Nigel also sprang down and moved quickly across the ice, although Nigel was far in the rear.

The others watched, holding their breath, as the boys disappeared from sight over the far side of the icy upheavals, huge chunks of ice thrown together by the tide. One by one the men also passed from view as the others waited anxiously in the sleigh.

On the far side of the ridge, Reginald raced across the ice, heading toward the edge, determined to be able to say that he had seen the very edge of Freezeland Street, and Theodore ran just behind him.

"Let's slow down, Reg!" Theo called. "Go to it slowly!"

Just then the ice gave way beneath Reginald, and he shot through the opening, arm upstretched.

Nineteen

In the sleigh, Olivia, convinced that the worst was happening beyond the ridge of ice, appeared about to faint, while Elise, unable to remain still when she might be able to help, had gotten down to follow the others.

"You will find Olivia's vinaigrette in her muff, Mr. Gray," she said briskly. "Wave it beneath her nose a few times and she'll soon revive."

Then she pulled a lap robe from the sleigh, informing the driver that she would be back it with directly and, ignoring his protests, turned to hurry across the ice in the direction of the others. She was joined by Arthur Townsend, who, abandoned for the majority of the day, had finally spotted them in the sleigh. He had come loping down City Road after them, and now accompanied Elise to see if he could be of service.

When they reached the top of the ice ridge, they saw a human chain stretched across the ice toward Reginald. Theo, lying flat on the ice, had grabbed Reggie's hand, Monty had grabbed Theo's feet to keep him from being pulled in, Belvedere was lying with a grip on Monty's boots, and Nigel was serving as the anchor.

"Hold on to him and pull, Theo!" Monty was shouting. "The ice'll give way if the rest of us come any closer!"

Theo dutifully pulled and Monty reeled Theo in, as though he were the fishing line and Reggie the fish on the end of it. As the ice cracked ahead of them, the others slid carefully back, bringing the two boys with them and retreating to the safety of the ridge. There Elise wrapped the lap robe around the half-frozen Reginald, and Mr. Belvedere picked him up and all but ran back to the sleigh.

"Take us to the closest fire!" he ordered the driver as the others piled in.

The sleigh moved briskly back into the city of tents and drew up in front of one that housed a coffeehouse.

"Accident, Caleb!" shouted the driver to the proprietor within. "Boy broke through the ice!"

Belvedere carried Reginald in, barking orders as he went. Soon several braziers were pulled together and more coal heaped in them. The men removed their greatcoats and held them up as a screen, both to hold the warmth in around the fire and to provide Reginald with a trace of privacy as Belvedere rapidly stripped off his wet clothes and boots, scrubbed him down with a rough cloth the proprietor had handed him and wrapped him in his own greatcoat. Elise and Mr. Townsend had been dispatched to find a booth selling clothing—for they had everything at the fair—and find something for Reginald to wear.

By the time they had returned with their purchases, Reginald was looking slightly better, for he was beginning to thaw, and Monty had just poured a cup of hot coffee laced with brandy down his throat. Then, still behind the relative privacy of the screen of coats, they got Reginald dressed and wrapped up in a dry lap robe. At the promise of a very good rate, the sleigh had remained outside the tent, ready to carry Reginald back to their carriage.

"No need in everyone coming," Monty announced. "Take him home ourselves, and the rest of you stay until it's over for the evening."

Nigel, eager to be on his way home, hurried back into his greatcoat, prepared to head toward the sleigh.

"Are you certain, Monty?" asked Elise doubtfully. "I hate to see you go while we stay to have a good time."

"We must expect to make sacrifices, cousin," Nigel assured her, patting her shoulder. "This is just one of those good times that Monty and I must give up for the sake of the family."

"I'll come with you," announced Arthur Townsend. "I might be of some service to you, and I'd only be a third wheel here." He turned to bow to Elise and Olivia, as well as the two remaining gentlemen.

"I searched for your scarf, Miss Olivia," he said, "but I fear there was no sign of it."

Livy had the grace to blush, but she held out her hand and said, "It was very chivalrous of you to look for it, sir."

He bowed low over her hand and, it seemed to Elise, he held himself considerably taller as he turned to climb into the sleigh.

The four of them stood there and watched the sleigh pull away, then let out a collective sigh.

"I believe that it is more than time for us to dine," said Mr. Gray. "I know that it is early still by our normal standards, but this is surely not a normal day. And around us," he added, pointing, "night is already falling."

And it was true. The winter night was falling suddenly and coldly, as winter nights often do. Already torches were being lighted so that the fairgoers could find their way among the tents.

They made their way to the tent where Elise and Mr. Gray had stopped the day before because Elise had mentioned to Olivia that the young man who sang there had a wonderful voice, and she was eager to hear him. After the excitement of the last two hours, the tent seemed a haven of peacefulness. They found a table close by a glowing brazier and were untroubled by the smell of the tallow candles that provided the only other lighting, for the tent was filled with the fragrance of rosemary and thyme and roasting meat.

"Here he is, Livy," said Elise, nodding toward the young man who had taken his place in a corner of the tent, holding a lute and tuning it gently. Mr. Belvedere, she noticed, had gone to speak to him and had given him a coin. A kind gesture, she thought.

To their delight, he began with an old favorite, his mellow voice filling the tent and making even the most hardened of listeners pause to listen to its sweetness.

> *Alas, my love, you do me wrong*
> *To cast me off discourteously*
> *And I have loved you so long*
> *Delighting in your company.*
>
> *Greensleeves was all my joy*
> *Greensleeves was my delight*
> *Greensleeves was my heart of gold*
> *And who but my Lady Greensleeves.*

The crowd listened, transfixed, until he reached the end of the last chorus, and then they erupted into applause, convincing him by a shower of silver to sing it again. This time many of them sang the chorus with him each time.

"Have you a gown with green sleeves, Miss MacGregor?" murmured Mr. Belvedere, leaning close to her during one particularly heartfelt delivery of the chorus.

"I believe so, sir. Why do you ask?" she replied.

"How very suitable," he responded. "Perhaps you might wear it for me tomorrow."

She glanced up at him, her eyebrows high. "And why would I do that, Mr. Belvedere?" she inquired.

"Why, because I asked you to do so, ma'am, and I am your affianced husband."

She frowned. "You assume a great deal too much, sir."

The song ended before they could continue, and the applause and conversation of the crowd made conversation impossible for a while. They listened to three or four more ballads, and then Mr. Gray suggested that they make their way to a barge frozen in the ice, which he had noticed earlier in the day. It had displayed a sign announcing that there would be music and dancing there that evening, and he proposed that they attend.

To the delight of the ladies, the barge was lighted with torches planted in the snow and fiddlers were warming their instruments. As they took their places for a quadrille, Elise murmured, "It seems to me that I recall the last ball we attended together, Mr. Belvedere."

"I am pleased to see that your memory has not forsaken you, ma'am," he replied.

"And you appeared to feel that I was quite nonsensical, enjoying both the dance and the conversation."

"I would never have thought *you* nonsensical, Miss MacGregor," he assured her, "although I might have felt some doubt about the conversation."

"I believe that you found fault with a compliment paid me," she continued.

"Not the compliment, but the manner in which it was conveyed, ma'am," he responded.

The dance separated them at that point and, when they were together once more, she asked, "Why do you think me feather-witted, sir?"

He glanced down at her, genuinely startled. "Feather-witted? I don't believe I recall ever saying that to you, Miss MacGregor."

"Not in precisely those words, perhaps, but you have certainly conveyed to me the feeling that you think me light-minded and careless."

They were about to be separated by the movement of the dance, and he said, "When this dance has ended,

ma'am, perhaps you might do me the favor of granting
me a private conversation."

She inclined her head graciously. "As you wish."

When the dance had drawn to a close, he drew her
away to the shadowy bow of the barge. "I think perhaps
you have misunderstood me, Miss MacGregor," he said
earnestly, looking down into her eyes.

Elise, finding his closeness a little unsettling and remembering their kiss in the library, said, "Indeed, sir?"
Then she railed at herself inwardly, asking herself if that
was the very best she could do as repartee.

"Indeed," he assured her, drawing a little closer. "Did
you listen to the song, Miss MacGregor?"

"The song?" she asked blankly, thinking of the music
for the quadrille.

"'Greensleeves,'" he replied. "The song the young man
sang when we first arrived for dinner. Did you listen to it?"

"Naturally I listened. And of course I know the song.
Everyone does."

"I asked him to sing it," he said, "for you."

"For me?" she responded, startled. "Why for me?"

"Because of the first stanza and the chorus, ma'am,"
he replied, drawing her close to him. "I have not loved
you long because I have known you for only a fortnight,
but I swear to you that I *shall* love you long—and it is
true that I delight in your company, when I have never
delighted in the company of others."

Here he crushed her to him with such force that she
could scarcely breathe and kissed her until she most certainly could not. Strange, she thought, that the sensation
could seem so pleasant. Suddenly everything seemed so
correct, so absolutely as it should be. She didn't want a
man like James Gray, attached to his club and doing
everything as it should be done. She wanted a man who
cared deeply about something—and who would never

give her false coin. She could always trust him to say what he meant.

She wanted Walter Belvedere.

"I know that you are willful, ma'am," he said, when he at last let her draw a breath, "but I wish to say something to you despite that."

Willful, she thought. She had never been called willful in her life. She had always done precisely what was expected of her. And he had the power to anger her, to make her feel deeper emotions than she ever had. She thought about it a moment, and it occurred to her that she liked it. She would prefer to feel deeply rather than to be always calm.

"I have been to the goldsmith, Miss MacGregor," he began.

"I congratulate you, sir," she responded lightly. "I hope that you had a pleasant visit there."

"I did," he persevered. "I asked him to make something for me, and I wish to give it to you."

"To me?" she asked, her eyes wide. "I am relieved you went to the goldsmith then, sir."

He looked at her, his dark brows drawn together. "Why do you say that, ma'am?"

"Why, because, sir, you told me that you would never give me false coin," she responded demurely.

To her amazement, he laughed, a deep, rolling laugh that could be heard the length of the barge and more. Elise felt inordinately pleased. She had made Walter Belvedere laugh when, heaven knows, he had probably not laughed since he was a child.

When all was calm once more, he looked down at her with a surprisingly tender gaze. "Here, ma'am, is what I would like to give you, should you wish to accept it," he said, opening her hand and placing something in the palm of her glove. Elise opened it, and there lay a lovely gold ring, engraved with two clasped hands. She stared down at it, and then up at his hopeful face.

"But it is a betrothal ring," she said. "You told me that when you showed me your sketches."

He nodded, smiling. "In a day or two, Miss MacGregor, rain will come again and melt away the ice and snow, and put an end to the Frost Fair."

"Yes," she agreed, "naturally it will not last. Frost Fairs never do."

"I would prefer that our engagement not end with the fair, ma'am," he said gently, leaning forward to kiss her once more.

"The ring is engraved, although you cannot read it in this flickering torchlight," he told her, when she emerged once more from his embrace.

"What does it say?" she asked him.

"It says 'To my delight, my heart of gold,'" he said, pulling her close once more. "Will you wear it, ma'am?"

She smiled, and when she had kissed him once more, she took off her glove so that he could slip it on her finger. "I shall wear it till I die, Mr. Belvedere," she said.

When their carriage arrived in Darlington Square, the gentlemen escorted them in, and they were startled to find all the household up, and all gathered in the drawing room—with the exception of the young children and Reginald.

"Reginald is going to be all right, is he not?" asked Elise, concerned by this late gathering.

"Oh yes," said Lucy. "Thanks to Monty and Nigel and Mr. Belvedere, he will be quite well again. I have thanked Monty and Nigel for saving my son, but, Mr. Belvedere, I have not yet thanked you, sir."

And to the shock of those who had just entered the

room, she walked over to Mr. Belvedere, stood on her toes, and kissed his cheek.

Elise stared at Monty and he shrugged. "Happy to have him home safe," he said.

Suddenly Elise realized that they had people other than those in their family circle, for Livy jabbed her in the ribs. She glanced up and there stood Mr. Robert Westbrook, looking directly at her.

"Miss MacGregor," he said, coming forward with his hand outstretched, "I am pleased to see you looking so well."

"Thank you, Mr. Westbrook," she responded with what composure she could muster. "I am surprised to see you here in London."

"I came as soon as I knew that you had decided to break off our engagement," he responded, and Elise glanced up sharply to meet Ravinia's calm gaze. Her aunt shook her head slightly, so Elise said nothing.

"I began my journey here with the intent of changing your mind, Miss MacGregor," he said, "but I must confess that I had my mind changed instead."

Elise stared at him, puzzled. "I'm sorry, Mr. Westbrook, but I'm not certain that I understand."

He nodded his head, smiling. "I'm not certain that I do either, but I must tell you, ma'am, that I also find myself engaged to someone else, and I hope you will forgive me."

Elise stared at him. "You are engaged, sir?" she asked.

He nodded, smiling. "I did not plan for it to happen, but I do indeed find myself engaged to Miss Ivy Sterling, who has asked me to give you her best regards, and to request that you come to call upon her as soon as we are married."

"I believe that you may assure her I will do so," replied Elise, smiling. "And I wish you very happy, sir."

"I understand that I should do the same, ma'am," he

said, and for an instant Elise froze. Was he about to congratulate her upon being engaged to James Gray?

Over Mr. Westbrook's shoulder, she again caught Ravinia's eye.

"Would like to be the one to introduce you, Mr. Westbrook," said Monty. "This is Mr. Walter Belvedere, Elise's fiancé."

"My congratulations, sir," said Westbrook, bowing.

"And mine to you, sir," replied Belvedere.

As Elise and Olivia prepared for bed that evening, Livy said, "Are you truly happy, Elise?"

Her sister nodded, smiling. "Truly, my dear," she said. "Do you mind?"

Livy looked shocked for a moment, then said, "Do you mean because I said I liked Mr. Belvedere? Well, I do, you know. He is a very kind man, and if you are fond of him, I shall be happy for you, but I could never be interested in the sort of life he lives."

Elise breathed a sigh of relief and continued brushing her hair.

After a minute or two had passed, Livy said, "Did you notice how generous and helpful Mr. Townsend was today?"

"I did indeed," agreed Elise, smiling.

Livy sighed. "I do like him so much," she said.

Elise turned the gold ring on her finger and smiled again. "And so do I," she said. "So indeed do I."

As she lay awake that night, Elise heard the gentle sound of falling rain. The wind had shifted to the south, the temperature had risen, and rain now fell instead of snow. The Frost Fair was at an end, but her Frost Fair engagement was not.

She smiled in contentment. Her life was just beginning.

Epilogue

"Do hurry, Freddie," called Muriel Belvedere to her husband.

"I am coming as quickly as I can," he assured her.

"Well, we certainly would not wish to miss little Monty's christening," she reminded him. She stopped a moment and looked up at her husband. "I still cannot believe that this is true. Walter is married and has a son."

"Two daughters, too," Freddie reminded her as they hurried into the carriage. "If he keeps it up, we shall soon have so many grandchildren that I won't be able to recall their names."

"Nonsense, Freddie," she laughed. "You know that you are as excited as I am. At last you have an heir!"

Her husband smiled broadly and nodded, but then he added, "But you know, my dear, I still have trouble understanding some of the things that Walter says to me."

"What do you mean, Freddie? Give me an example," she replied.

"Well, just yesterday I asked him what he was going to do to celebrate Monty's christening, and he said that he and Elise plan to go to the nearest fair. Sometimes I think that he has been spending far too much time with Monty Longfellow. Can't understand a word he says."

Muriel smiled and patted his hand. "What does it matter, Freddie? Six years ago, who would ever have guessed that Walter would be a happy husband and father?"

Freddie looked down at her tenderly. "We are very fortunate, my dear."

At the christening, Muriel was greatly struck by how lovely her daughter-in-law looked. She was wearing a gown of green trimmed with gold, and her sleeves were long. As she held her son, Monty, at the altar, music played softly from the shadows, a secular tune. After a moment, Muriel could identify it.

Greensleeves was all my joy
Greensleeves was my delight
Greensleeves was my heart of gold
And who but my Lady Greensleeves.